STAGE TO AMARILLO

by

Dick Coler

"THE STAGE TO AMARILLO" is a Western novel of purely fiction-depicting events that may have occurred during the Kiowa/Comanche Indian uprisings. The Kwahadie clan of Comanche is sometimes spelled as Quahadie. The characters and some places are the product of the author's imagination or are used only fictitiously, and any resemblance to actual persons, living or dead, any business establishments, events or some locales is entirely coincidental.

Order this book online at www.trafford.com
or email orders@trafford.com

Most Trafford titles are also available at major online book retailers.

Printed in the United States of America.

ISBN: 978-1-4269-7029-0 (sc)
ISBN: 978-1-4269-7030-6 (e)

Trafford rev. 05/14/2011

 www.trafford.com

North America & international
toll-free: 1 888 232 4444 (USA & Canada)
phone: 250 383 6864 ♦ fax: 812 355 4082

-dedicated to all my ridin' pals-of all ages-
especially the ones with whom I've been
privileged to 'ride the river.'

CHAPTER 1

She stubbed her old cigarette in the small, porcelain ash tray and carried it with her into the kitchen and placed it on the window sill above the sink, and turned and lit another one.

The cat, in its calico coat, purred as it arched its back and rubbed its lithe body against her leg as it was weaving between her feet. Kate opened the door to the ice box and took out the bottle with the cream that was separated when the skim-milk calves were fed, and poured some into a saucer for Elizabeth.

That done, she raised up and flicked the ash off her cigarette into that same porcelain ash tray on the window sill and started to wash her hands with the cake of lye soap that lay in its own dish next to the edge of the kitchen sink.

The cord-wood used to fuel the stove was almost gone from the wood box and she hoped there would be enough to last through supper without having to split any more.

The wind was urging the blue-black clouds to dance across the range, and it caused them to dip lower where they could eventually pour out rain to drench the fields that would welcome it; soaking in as quickly as it fell.

The temperature adjusted to the conditions and was cooling rapidly. Elstun guessed that by the time he drove the team to the end of the field, he'd better then turn back to the barn.

He had all the hay but about an acre raked and windrowed and most of the west end of that parcel was stacked already. He thought that with just one more full day all fourteen acres would be stacked and prepared for any early weather that was certain to make an appearance at this time of the year.

"Gee, Rafe, Gee, Dan." He slapped at the reins as he spoke to the sorrel team of horses hitched to the double-tree of an old McCormick hay rake. The team made a right turn and both easily hauled the equipment toward the end of the field at the barn, where they had first entered.

In less than ten minutes he unhitched the rake and the team was driven in the old and weathered barn. Each animal was unharnessed and each collar and harness-rein and head stall was placed in its collective state at the end of each stall. Each horse was then freed to water at a side trough and enter back to its own extra wide stall, to relax and begin to eat. A few cobs of field corn were provided as well as some flakes of hay for ol' Rafe and Dan.

The first gigantic roll of thunder was preceded only seconds before with a huge and sparkling crack of lightning, but the team stood placidly eating. They were little disturbed by the sounds of nature and the ensuing storm, now in its full force.

Biff and Dusty, the red-bone and the blue-tick hound dogs, were over in the corner of the barn where they usually quartered, awaiting the team to return denoting their supper time, and were soon duly rewarded.

Elstun Calhoon was nearly soaked with rain as he approached the back of the white, frame house and stood on the recently poured sand and gravel stoop that acted as a catch-all for debris that carried toward the house from the corrals.

A year or so ago he'd put some corrugated pieces of metal on top of the vigas extending out from the back entrance, thus enabling him to clean his boots or shed his gear while outside under cover. The raindrops were dancing to an acoustical echo that was shouting its blasphemy of water-power on the metal-covered roof.

Kate hollered from the kitchen when she heard noises from the back entrance.

"Is 'at-chew, Elstun?"

"Yeah, it is."

"Well, it didn't sound like ya."

"Yeah, well, it is me."

"I thought it war mebby them dern ol' hounds o'yourn a-tryin to git in outer the rain."

"Naw, it warn't, hit war . . ."

"Elizabeth ain't through her supper yet and I don't want them ol' hounds inside mah house."

"Kate, hit's jes me, and I'm a-comin' inside cuz I'm wet plumb through. Them dawgs is still a-feedin' in the barn."

"Now, Elstun, you know better'n to walk nekked through mah kitchen."

"I ain't nekked. I got mah drawers on, and I'm a-fixin' to get on some dry duds. I swear, Kate, you arter be bored fer the simples, way you carry on."

"Now hurry up, Els, the biscuits is near done and I'm 'bout outa stove-wood,"

"Wished you'd told me afore I tuck off mah britches, I'd-a split you s'more."

"Never mind," Kate replied, "it kin jes wait'll after supper. Now, git!"

The storm was urging more water on the small ranch the Calhoon's took over from Kate's mother after that awful day.

Comanche and Kiowas joined forces to raid all the new settlements from the Oklahoma territory in the western part of the panhandle, south into Texas, about as far as the Canadian river. Seven families were killed and most buildings burned and their livestock butchered or captured.

Kate's father and brother were slain and Kate just never fully recovered her senses after she and her mother escaped by hiding in an escarpment of rocks near the creek that ran through the property.

The thirty years that passed since she was eleven were wrought with hardship trying to help with the upkeep of the big ranch. The deed was recorded in Hartley county in an area between the Rita Blanca and the Punta de Agua rivers, seventy miles from Oklahoma.

Elstun Calhoun was the only cowhand working for the ranch when the Indians raided the area, and Silas had sent him to Hutchinson county to bring back a team of work horses Kate's dad purchased from his cousin in Skellytown.

Elstun was ten years older than Kate and always had a fondness for her, mostly because she seemed so grown-up, and then, too, she was a comely young girl and she adored the young cowboy. They married the year Kate turned thirteen, and she bore a son the following year. Two weeks later her mother passed and Kate's mind started to recede in each passing month.

Barton Daniel Calhoon, almost twenty-seven, hadn't been back to the old ranch homestead for over two years, and he was anxious to get back home to Hartley county.

CHAPTER 2

Bart knew his daddy was quite capable of operating the ranch in the semi-farm land without his help, but now that his dad was in his fifties, he thought perhaps the right thing to do would be to talk him into hiring a hand for most of the heavy chores. Besides, he was aware of the condition of his mother and he wanted them to both meet his new wife he'd found and married when he was in old Mexico, in the state of Chihuahua, in the village of Ojinaga.

Bart was working in Fort Stockton, Texas, after he'd served two years with the Army, where he was in a procurement section for the quartermaster, and he dealt with the cotton processors of the textile industry. He decided that the cattle and the horses could wait since he'd almost had his fill of this cowboy work before he went into the U.S. Army.

Involvement in the textile business took him south to the border town of Presidio, Texas, where a mill was built and Mexican labor was used to operate it.

It was here that Bart met Rosalita once when he'd crossed to Ojinaga. The first time they met she and her younger sister were dancing in the cantîna and she agreed to have a refreshment with the handsome cowboy.

The second time, a few days later, they walked together in the garden, with her ever-present guardian tîa (aunt) nearby. They talked of the town of Presidio, and the textile mill located there, and his job with the company. This evening, when Bart entered the cantîna, he seated himself at one of the tables in the back. He saw Rosa's fiery eyes seek him out, and awaited her song to end before he made his way toward her, past the end of the hand-made, cottonwood bar, and past the glassy stares of the obreros, tilting their bottles of tequilas and habénaro and cervésa. He was certain now, she was one of the most beautiful women he had ever seen.

"Ah, señor, la señorita es precio cien pesos," said the patron, smirking.

"One hundred pesos!" Bart answered in an astonished state. "Who are you?" he added. "I only wish to speak with her again. You see, *Señor, sé llama, ella es Rosalita,* an we've known each other for some time now. You must be new here, I've never seen you before, so, *våmanos."*

She was gorgeous. She smelled of the evening lilacs, and contrary to custom, she spoke first.

"No Español, Bart. I say *Inglis.* All thees time chu and I visit together, tîå mia ees weeth us, or very nearby."

She smiled and she exposed the most beautiful teeth Bart felt he'd ever seen; a full-lipped, round mouth, with a shiny completion of light olive. Her breasts were full and tight as they pressed into the white, hand-embroidered blouse with the symbols of her name, red roses.

Bart found himself standing up and rolling-a-cob with his boot as he spoke with a stammer.

"Y-You're very beautiful, Rosa, and I'm falling in love with you."

"B-Bart, oh, Bart Cal-hoon, *tî amo,* Bart. I am falling for love for chu, too.

"Bart ees such a-a different name, ees eet your Christian name; what you are reely called, Señor?"

"N-no, just Bart," he said. I guess it's a short name for Barton . . . I know that's what my folks named me; Barton Daniel Calhoon. Sounds loco, don't it?"

They both laughed, and Bart was very surprised that this beautiful girl wasn't shy about her approach to him. Her forthright greeting in this crude and rustic *tabérna* caused him to question her motive.

"Eet's very simple, Señor Bart, each gringo that comes here, which ees not very soon, wants only one thing on hees mind. Pablo tells me chu are work weeth Tejånøs een Presidio, and I wish to leave thees place to find good work in that Texas meel."

The music started again, and she did not leave her spot next to the tall Texan. Her younger sister, Conchita, left her side and began to sing and clap her hands and stomp her feet to the festive music.

"Rosa, why don't we s . . ."

"*Mi amigo, Pablo,* say chu are not like all the other Gringos who come here. He say he remember chu from two times before and chu only come here for the *cervésa* y *la müsica.'*

She placed her hand in his and led him to a small table nearer the door in a small room in the back.

"Pablo was right, at least 'til now, and you are just so beautiful, all I want is to watch you and talk with you, I . . ."

She interrupted him again, and said; "Walk weeth me, out here een thees påtio, and tell me about who chu reely are, and what chu reely want weeth me."

"I must admit," Bart said, while he fumbled for the right words, "I wasn't prepared for this kind of evening. You've completely captured my heart. I will take you with me across the border, but are you certain you want to go to work in Presidio, in the cotton mill?"

He stood and waited for her answer, and when she stopped he gently pulled her to his side and their lips met within the seconds it took to embrace.

"Did you allow me to kiss you so that I will take you to Texas?"

Her answer was an ardent grasp of his tall body and a placement of her red, moist lips, parted against his. Her torn heart beat rapidly and her body heaved with emotion as she repeatedly kissed him and welcomed his tender response. "No, Bart, no. I do not geeve myself because of any thoughts of crossing to the *Estådos* weeth chu. I suddenly find my heart to be alone weeth chu and spend a lifetime together. I wish to hol' chu next to me. I weel cook for chu and take care of chu and follow where ever chu'll go. I weel bring in hoppines."

Bart sat on a nearby wooden bench to gather up his thoughts.

When Rosalita looked around at the back-lit shadow that was cast on the Satîllo tile of the påtio floor, she saw Conchita. She was leaning against an alabaster wall. It was covered with red and yellow roses, and it emitted a faded blue reflection from the cantîna lights inside. Her sister was tenderly wiping the few tears from her cheek as she quickly disappeared.

Bart looked up at Rosalita and said quietly, "I will take you with me tonight if you are willing, but first I must find one I should speak with to ask for your hand in marriage."

"I only have *dos familia* - two people, Bart, weeth whom I dearly love. *Hermana mia, Conchita, y tia mia, Anita.* We both stay weeth my *tia* Anita, and it becomes harder to feed everyone, since our parents are died. My seester weel take care of our aunt, and she will bless our union. My aunt will wish to meet chu and she, too, weel understand my love for chu and my decision to depart."

"It's settled then," Bart replied. "We'll go to your home now, together, and you can gather your personals, and we'll leave tonight for the border. I know the exact place where we can be married, The preacher-man always has his church open, and I've known him for a long time. He'll take care of us both, and you and I can be married in Presidio. I know it's quick but I also know this is the best way . . . once we've decided."

She clung to his side, and her knees started to weaken, and her heart beat even faster as she pointed the direction to her small *haciénda.*

A quick glance at the door for her sister resulted in Conchita hurriedly leaving the *tabérna* with a smile and misting eyes.

It was still early in the evening when they said their teary goodbyes and left the land down below, where the little piñons grow, and headed for Texas and the start of their life together.

Bart explained to his beautiful, new wife, after a night and a day in this old border town hotel, how his decision to return home to Hartley county and his old home ranch was paramount in his thoughts.

Bart bought a mule to carry their packs and an extra horse, for Rosalita, and they set off for Fort Stockton, Texas. Bart thought it was a little over two hundred miles to Lubbock, and about another hundred miles or so to Amarillo.

He decided he'd sell the mule when they reached Fort Stockton, and there get tickets on the stage coach to Lubbock.

CHAPTER 3

They tethered their mounts behind the stage coach on their way to Lubbock, and would do the same at the change in Amarillo, then pick-up another pack-horse there, to ride home.

The year was 1872, and the late war between the states was still a major sore spot with most of the Texans who were in the majority as Southern sympathizers.

Bart served with the New Mexico detachment of regulars at Fort Sumner in De-Baca county, ranging south to Carlsbad and the Texas border and west to present day Albuquerque.

The Kwahadie Comanche were the main source of problems east of Fort Sumner, and further west dwelt the Lipan and the Mescalero Apache. Bart's time was spent mostly breaking horses for the remount station at Fort Sumner.

He was involved with two major skirmishes and five minor ones during his two-year hitch.

The United States Government in general, and the Federal Bureau of Indian Affairs in particular, were being chastised by the eastern newspapers and the bureaucrats regarding the mishandling of the Indian insurrections through out the western territories.

The railroads were waging a battle in the house of representatives, and the mining companies were lobbying in the senate. General Crook was involved in the Indian pursuits of the Apache in Arizona and western New Mexico, and the raiding was still being done by many members of these tribes as well as the northern plains tribes.

General Sheridan's campaign was over in the north, and General Sherman dispatched Colonel Archie McBride and two Army regiments to Nacodoches, in east Texas.

The Kwahadie Comanche and the Kiowa to the north of the Texas panhandle were still the denizens of this part of Texas, and they ranged all the way from the Guadalupe mountains in eastern New Mexico to western Oklahoma, and south beyond the Antelope mountain range near San Angelo.

Peace on the frontier was never more tenuous. The treaty of 1868 set up reservations for the Cheyennes, Arapahos, and some Kiowas and Comanches, but most of the Indians refused to settle on the reservations, and since congress was involved with the impeachment proceedings of President Johnson, it did not follow through with the necessary funds to meet government treaty obligations.

Even as late as 1876-7, when many of the Sioux Indian bands fled to Canada, most all those northern tribes were still in a fight that would end with the stabbing of Crazy Horse by a soldier in Camp Robinson, in Nebraska.

In spite of the government to establish reservations and step up proceedings to stop the sporadic raids of many tribes, the Comanche was not entirely defeated, and posed a threat to the many travelers in wayward areas between destinations. So was the case on a Thursday evening as the stage carrying Bart and his bride, all too soon would encounter.

Doctor Wayne Mullins was one of the passengers on the Carrington Brothers Stage and Transport Company. The six-up was being driven by H.R. "Lynx" Walters, and his partner riding shotgun was old man Parker, who made his home in Lubbock. Rosalita was sitting next to her new husband and was holding his head on her shoulder, content in her decision to marry and go home with Bart to Hartley county. Bart was sleeping soundly, in spite of the rough ride the large stage coach was making on its forty mile route to the sand hills near Kermit, Texas. This was about ten miles from the New Mexico border, and the first planned stop for the dusty stage coach.

Wade Parker saw them first, off to the east, maybe a mile away and moving toward the stage. He pointed and pounded Lynx on the shoulder, then leaned over to alert the passengers inside.

"Injuns, folks! And I count about twelve or thirteen. Hold on, it's only about three miles to the Kermit's station and Lynx thinks we can make a run for it."

Bart was immediately awake and another of the passengers, a west Texas cowboy on a horse buying trip from a ranch over west by Saratoga, was already crawling through the side window to settle on a shooting spot from a perch atop the stage coach.

Bart instantly looked back to see how the two saddle horses tied to the back of the stage were making it. Their saddles were stored on top and they were tied with their halter ropes, and seemed to be all right. He thought of cutting them loose, and that maybe the Indians would settle for two horses, and then . . . decided against that idea.

Doc Mullins had a disassembled shot gun that he was busy putting together, and he indicated he had a box of fifty shells setting on the floor. The fifth passenger was a soldier's wife on the way to meet her husband in Portales, New

Mexico, territory. She'd catch a different stage in Lubbock for her last hundred miles.

She was very frightened, but said not a word. Rosalita moved over in the seat where the cowboy left, and attempted to comfort her.

CHAPTER 4

Comanches, Indians of the Shoshone or Snake tribe, were called "The Lords of the Plains." perhaps the fiercest of these tribes were the Kwahadie Comanche. Being expert equestrians, they were more at home on their pony's backs than they were afoot, for they all learned to ride and handle their horses at a very early age.

One trick, at which they were particularly adept, was to place one leg secured with a hair rope, used as a foothold, over their pony's back and sliding under the neck of the horse to dispense their arrows from very short bows.

These Indians had seldom, if ever, seen any firearms, which they called "Thunder-sticks." They carried clubs and some lances, but always many arrows and a small, strong bow which was much easier to handle in a fight while mounted. Long bows and long arrows were for hunting.

Not only were the Comanche skilled riders, they were also ruthless killers.

All the Indians were screaming and yipping with the sound the coyote makes when he's on a kill, and still out of range to loose their arrows.

One warrior, riding a larger and faster than average Overo pinto, was far in front of the band racing toward the stagecoach. He was heading on a diagonal line toward the six coach horses.

"Haw, Babe, haw, Belle," said Lynx, as he shouted to the lead team of mares, insisting they turn a sharp left and head into the oncoming brave. The swing team and the wheel horses followed.

Old man Parker was delighted with the move as he deepened his seat and took careful aim, now that he had an open shot over the horses at the Comanche.

He carried a Sharps repeating rifle and two Walker Colt pistols. The Sharps barked a single time and that warrior threw up his arms as he instantly tumbled, heels up, off the pony's back. He bounced twice on the desert floor with a claret-colored hole in his chest, and his arrows strewn around his body.

Suddenly, the warriors split, and half veered hard to their left to better position themselves on the right side of the stage, while the rest peeled off to their right. They were closer now and their screams and yelling were continuing to haunt the wary passengers.

Bart tried to explain to Rosalita and the soldier's wife that their yelling was done to give themselves ample courage.

Two of the redskins made a poor decision to approach the right side of the coach too closely. It put them within about thirty yards and a perfect range for Doc Mullins' shotgun.

The noise reverberating inside the coach was deafening, and the result was exactly as hoped. Pellets landed in a small pattern on the first brave and blew him off his horse as a tremendous force of wind would blow away a tumbleweed.

Some of the shot struck the white mare the second brave was riding and her eye and jaw were filled with pellets. She fell in a heap as the cowboy up top was sending a cartridge into the falling Indian.

Smoke was curling, tall and black, from the Kermit station, as the stage was closing the distance.

Bart missed with his first shot, but he fired his .44-.40 again and this time hit a Comanche in the thigh. Bart thought the Indian fell at the shot, but instead, he pulled the trick of sliding under the horse's neck to wield his arrows. The warrior was getting too close to the stage coach teams, and Bart reacted quickly by snapping off another shot that struck the Indian in his shoulder and dropped him to the ground.

Two of the Comanche circled wide around the back side of the stage and were attempting to reach the two saddle horses tied to the rear. They most likely didn't shoot them because they'd lost three horses already and could use them.

Bart spied them the same time the cowboy on top of the coach did. They both fired at the trailing Indians and they both hit the same one simultaneously. The other Indian reined up his pony and rapidly pulled away.

Inside the coach, Rosalita pointed to the smoke she saw rising from the nearby sand hills and the way station nestled there. It was apparent there had been a skirmish and the corral had been set on fire, likely by these same Indians.

The coach horses were racing with the stage and narrowing the distance to the station, with the driver urging them forward. Bart was concentrating on another of the warriors, riding a Tobiano pinto, carrying a feathered lance and a triple-skin buffalo shield.

The Indian was trailing the stage and attempting to hurl the lance up over the back and into the front where Lynx and Wade were.

The instant the lance was thrown, Bart fired his .44-.40 pistol and knocked the Indian, mortally wounded, from the pinto pony. The west Texas cowboy thumbed the hammer back on his rifle about the same time, and split open the skull of yet another of the marauders, about fifty yards away from stage coach's side. The six that were left saw this and they quickly pulled rein and rode off.

The stage coach was nearly to its destination, as Lynx steadily pulled in the reins of the six-up teams, and called to the horses to slow down and circle toward the standing three buildings at the edge of the Kermit settlement. Everyone could see the smoldering corral as the stage coach slid to a halt.

Three horses in the corral were dead, one looked badly wounded, and two, frightened but unhurt, nervously stood at the far back side. The cowboy was climbing down the back of the coach as Bart exited its side door. Wade Parker climbed down and Doc Mullins got out, and they both ran back toward some rock out-croppings to act as a rear guard.

Lynx urged the team slightly closer to the first cabin, before he started to unhitch them and walk them to the water trough. He held them back as long as he could, feeling they'd cool down some before he'd allow them to drink.

The cowboy had already passed the charred logs of the corral, attempting to get some rope on the remaining horses, and inspecting the wounds of the gelding that was hurt.

Bart opened the door to the first cabin and entered. In the corner of the room, seated in a chair and barely able to move, was Harley Henderson, the man who was the station master, employed by the Carrington Brothers Stage Line.

The floor surrounding him and the floor by the corner window was strewn with empty cartridges. His two rifles and two unloaded pistols remained by his side.

As Bart approached him, he could see the three arrows in his chest. The blood had clotted around them and spilled over him and onto the floor below the window.

He told Bart his name and tried to explain what happened when he passed out from his injuries. There was no one else around and Bart called from the door to Rosalita for some help. She and the soldier's wife would tend to Henderson while Bart went back outside.

The cowboy had meanwhile reconstructed most of the corral and then he helped Lynx hitch the coach team of wheel horses to haul the other dead horses away from the scene.

There was plenty of provisions in the next cabin that was used as a commissary as well as extra harness and blankets, and a large supply of ammunition. Boxes of both long and short rounds, which would serve to reload both pistol and rifle. There was also box of patches.

Felicia Rogers, the soldier's wife, was considerably more calm and no longer seemed as frightened as when she was in the stage coach. She and Rosalita had become quite close amid their moments of peril, and she credited Rosalita for her fortitude.

Doc Mullins and old man Parker were still keeping watch about three hundred yards away from all the cabins. It was an uncertainty among Bart and Lynx and now the cowboy, who joined them, as to the plans of the surviving Comanches that abandoned them after the fight. Bart asked Walker Barnes, the cowboy from Saratoga, what his thoughts were.

"Like I said, Bart, I've not fought many of the Comanch', but it 'pears to me them Injun boys are likely to regroup up an prob'ly foller us here . . . whut you figure?"

"Not much doubt," chimed in Lynx, "that's the same bunch that made all this mess."

"Oh, yeah," said Bart, "I'm certain of it, and I agree they likely will come after us, but then again, they didn't have any guns to use, and they may figure our fire power is too strong."

"I imagine they snuck-up on ol' Harley, here. he shore put up a good fight, bein' all alone."

"They must've fired the corral and put arrows in them horses when he heered 'em an commenced to a-shootin," Lynx replied, rolling a long awaited smoke.

"Why do y'all reckon they rode out, 'stead of a-waitin' here to ambush us?" the young cowboy asked Bart.

"I figure they were jes too late with their doins here, else they would have stayed to make sure Mr. Henderson was alone and checked the other buildings. They no doubt saw us coming, and didn't want us to have all this cover."

Bart untied his grulla gelding and the mare he bought for Rosalita, and took them to the water trough near the corral.

"Looks as though there's enough hay on the other side of the corral, near the small shed, there," Lynx said to Bart. "I reckon we can feed all the horses now."

When the men finished they walked to the cabin where Harley Henderson was being tended to by Felicia and Rosalita, and who seemed to be feeling a whole lot better.

"Oh, Bart," Rosalita exclaimed, "Señor Hender-sohn tol' us there ees *mucha comida,* much food, een hees com-i-sary, een *la cabaña segúndo."*

"She means the second cabin, Missus Rogers, and I'd be obliged if you two ladies would fix us all something to eat."

"Looks like we'll all be here awhile, at least 'til tomorrow or when the horses is rested 'nuf to re-hitch, "Lynx announced. "Meantime, cowboy, let's you'n me go an spell Doc and ol' man Parker. Somebody's got to keep a eye on them Comanch'. Y'all kin come back and spell us after your a-done eatin', then we'll come up."

"We've a little time afore darkness sets on us," Bart replied. "If those redskins don't show up soon, I'll wager that they could wait 'til first light, 'specially since they have no guns. They'll need to make big medicine if they plan to raid us now that we're forted-up. Reckon we ought to start making up some plans to follow if we want to keep our hair.

About two hours passed and lateness started to produce the blackness that becomes totally encompassing in a land where lantern light or star an fire light is the only alternative,

Bart called to the men guarding the sand rock entrance to the station, to come in so they could all talk over plans. Wade Parker and Lynx Walters, since they worked for the stage line, had the final say in any plans. They agreed it was a good plan to put the ladies in the commissary cabin with Bart and Doc Mullins and the wounded stationer, along with Lynx and Wade Parker, in the first cabin, with the cowboy watching from the shed by the corral.

CHAPTER 5

Southeastern parts of Hartley county and northeastern Oldham county in the Texas panhandle west of Amarillo, was blessed with most of the two day rain.

The Rita Blanca and the Punta de Agua rivers overflowed their banks at the confluence of the east flowing Canadian. The Canadian river swelled to almost twice its normal size. Most folks guessed that almost six inches of rain fell.

Elstun was certainly glad he'd raked and stacked what he did, but he also figured he'd get a fifth cutting of his alfalfa, once the fields were dry enough to put the team in. He told Kate that he lost about an acre of fourth cutting.

"Hit's a-gittin' kindly airish outside 'bout now, ain't it, Els? 'Specially since that ol' winds a-come up, mebby we'll git some more of them ol' houms again."

"Kate, you referrin' to them mud-flats, or swampy places that dry up?"

"Yup."

"Well, they's onliest four's I knowed of, and they ain't that big, and I cain't grow nuthin' in there, anyways."

"We don't git these frog-stranglin' rains but 'bout onest a year," Kate answered.

"I know it. Shore greens up thangs fer a while. Heps the grass grow and makes for fat little calves. Onliest thang is, gotta watch out fer bogs, 'specially near our creek." Elstun used to pull bog when he was working in Colorado, before he came to work for Kate's father.

Kate was comfortably seated on the long sofa next to the table where one of the coal-oil lamps was emitting its acrid smell while it gave off only an adequate light. She sucked hard on the hand-rolled cigarette, and blew the smoke forward as she spoke to Elstun sitting in his cedar rocking chair.

"I 'member you a-tellin' me when I was a young thang, 'bout pullin' bog. Of how you'd rope them ol' steers and git yore horse too clost, an' a-gitin' him bogged, too. Better watch out, Els, you do thet today, you might bog under."

"Kate, I ain't got no intention ever of doin' that again," he sighed deeply at the thought. Elstun truly enjoyed the evenings in the ranch house, and the time he could spend with Kate. They liked to reminiscence and recall memories of past events, however trivial.

Elstun grew up in a poor environment, the son of Scottish immigrants who worked as a laborer and a cook on a ranch in eastern Colorado. His father was killed by an old cow he was doctoring, and when Elstun was twelve, he lost his mother to consumption.

He worked many years as a herdsman and cowboy, learning the profession and drifting to many ranches before he came to work for Kate's father, and stayed.

Kate had very little schooling, and captured the idiosyncrasies and ways of expression from hearing and speaking the dialect of her Kentucky born father and mother. They migrated to Oklahoma and eventually homesteaded the land in Texas until the Indian uprising that killed her father and her brother in 1839.

Kate, who had suffered through the years with anxiety attacks, due somewhat to the traumatic experiences when the Kiowa and Comanche warriors made their raids through the territory, was still a very handsome woman. She tried to keep herself looking good, although it took several years while Bart was growing up.

Kate desperately wanted another child, a little girl would've pleased her but it wasn't meant to be. She and Elstun worked very hard these past twenty-four years, and were very proud when their son passed through school.

They were even more proud and pleased when Bart announced he was going to try to go to a college in Ohio. He managed enough funds to remain for two years, and it was then he decided to return west and join the Army. He was able to pursue his love of reading during spare times, and wanted to help teach his parents to read better.

He sent books home and asked they be saved for when he would someday return home.

Kate and Elstun were excited when an overdue letter arrived from Bart one day " . . . *and soon we will all be together and I know you shall both be proud to meet my lovely wife.*"

"(signed) *BARTON DAN'L your loving son.*"

"Well, Kate, whadda ya' think o' that?"

"Read it agin, Els, that there part 'bout when they're a-leavin' Presidio, and 'bout when they're a-fixin' to git here. Ain't thet sumpin'? When was that writ?"

"Looks like the date on his letter says the twelfth, and this is the next to the last day of this month. Lessee, that's over a fortnight and a couple o'days. They should'a been here by now. 'Course, they maught got a mess o' thet rain we'ns did."

"Lordy, I hope not," mused Kate. Hit's past time to feed Elizabeth. I'll do thet rat now, whilst you tend to the stock."

"Kate."

"Whut?"

"Whar's the rest of them books Bart sent us, I thought they was in here?"

"Honey, you putt 'em in the box settin' thar beside the bedstead. Why?"

"I want to git 'em ready for Bart."

"Thet's a good idee, putt 'em whar we kin git to 'em easy enough, ever when we want to."

CHAPTER 6

The steel colored clouds were starting their ascent to the dark skies above, like an awning being lifted, and with it, rose the yellow and azure-blue of morning.

Doc Mullins finished changing the dressing on the shoulder of the wounded station man while Rosalita set the large, enamel-covered coffee pot on the stove to start to brew.

A rifle shot sang-out from the shed at the corral area, and then a second. Bart could see Walker Barnes from the slot through the closed shutters at the back window. Suddenly, there was gunfire from the first cabin where Lynx and Wade were holed-up.

It was difficult to see them, but Bart saw that there were many more of the Comanches than the six he counted when they let the stagecoach pull away to the station, yesterday. He thought now there were maybe about thirty Indians somewhere on the south and east side of the corral.

Lynx and Wade Parker were in the cabin about thirty yards from the shed at the back of the corral where the cowboy was stationed. Actually, the corall was set back about another twenty yards from the triangle it created. It afforded the two places a cross-fire effect should any Indian attempt to get at the corral.

It was obvious by now to everyone that the six warriors returned to their lodges later. Last night they likely made big medicine there, and enlisted more of their red warriors to assault the *Tosi-Tivo*, words they used for white man.

Walker Barnes was occupied watching one of the Comanche braves who was off his horse and attempting to creep, from rock by rock, toward the second cabin. The cowboy had to move quickly sideways to avoid a sudden thrust of a war club from another Indian he did not see, or hear.

The Indian slipped up to the side of the shed, and waited for Walker to start to reload before he rushed around the corner and in through the open door where Walker was stand-ing and attempting to reload.

The force knocked the cowboy over and into the corner of the shed, and he dropped the weapon he was reloading. The Kwahadie brave was painted with ochre and black across the lower portion of his face, and he was slashing out with his long knife at the chest of the fallen cowboy. Walker heard himself cry out at the pain before he actually felt the force of the blow at his forearm, raised to ward-off the nasty stab.

The shot was not heard by Walker as the Indian was lifted up and back to his tallest position, and pushed forward by the thrust of the shot to the back of his head. The cowboy looked up to see the back side of the warrior's face tear away.

The Comanche fell in a heap and the gristle and bone were mixed with the red ooze of blood gushing from his wound. In only seconds, Wade Parker suddenly showed himself in the doorway and grabbed the bloody, lifeless head of the Kwahadie warrior. He pulled his knife and snatched the blade across the forehead. there was a tearing sound and then a loud pop, as old man Parker avenged his wife's death. The Comanche that was inching his way toward the cabin where the ladies and Doc Mullins and the stationer were, was carefully being watched by Bart Calhoon.

There was a diversionary gallop by three painted Kwahadies' riding toward the center of the cabins toward the corral. It looked to the uninitiated that there were three ponies running at top speed with no riders on top.

Each Indian was leaning from the off shoulder of his horse, and shooting his arrows from under his pony's neck. Again, a Comanche trick performed to perfection.

A passel of arrows thunked into the outside logs and wooden door of the cabin as they pass, and at the release of the arrows, Doc Mullins threw open the door wide enough for him to fire both barrels of the shotgun at the renegades.

When the front horse and rider fell dead, the next was thrown and crippled by his own horse falling on him. The last rider attempted to pick up his comrade, but Harley Henderson, patched well by Doc Mullins, shot both from the pony, and fired again for the kill.

The Indian Bart was watching was concealed behind a deadfall about sixty feet from the cabin, as Rosalita made her way to the side window and spoke to her husband of five days.

"Thees Comanch' are very many, my hosban, chu must allow me now to use the pistola. I am a very good shoot."

"Rose, get down!" Bart demanded without turning, keeping his eyes on the Indian.

"But, *novio,* I can help chu, yes? I not afraid of the red mens."

The cedar arrow whizzed through the partly open shutter, deflected off the side , and nearly spent, buried itself in Rosalita's upper arm.

Doc Mullins sped to her side when he saw he fall to the nearby chair.

"Bart!" she cried out,

"Stay down," he repeated sternly, without once turning around.

She gasped, more embarrassed than badly hurt, and shyly managed a smile when she looked at the doctor.

"*Ah, médico, es nada, por esposa mia, aieee!*"

"Bart, C'mere a sec'," the doc said.

"Not now, Doc, I'm just about to get us another stinkin' red . . . hey! What th' hell happened?" He spun around and as quickly as he did, he moved to Rosalita.

"My God! Are you all right? How . . . "

"Ees *nada*, nothing my hosban'," she replied, as she saw the genuine care in the steel-gray eyes of her husband.

"Doc?"

"It looks worse than it is, Bart. I can get this shaft cut and the flint out with no trouble. No bones are broken, and it seems as if the deflection on the sill, there, had just about spent the arrow."

"Thank God. I'm sure glad it's not worse. Now, you just set tight while the doctor patches your arm, and stay back from the windows and the door. It goes for you, too, Missus Roberts."

The two shots caused everyone in the room to turn in time to see the station keeper whirl around with a wide grin on his face and smoke curling from his rifle.

"That one was probably your'n to kill Bart Calhoon, but I didn't think he was a-gonna wait for you to come back to the window."

Lynx Walters knew what his sidekick was going to do as soon as he saw him shoot the Indian that rushed the shed where the cowboy was holed-up. He also saw the red man that Barnes was watching, in front of the shed.

When the Indian showed himself at the sound of old man Parker racing to the shed, Lynx aimed his Sharps repeating rifle at the Comanche and watched him clutch his midsection as he dropped to the caliche ground.

"Let's all go to the second cabin with the rest," he exclaimed.

"I'd fret some 'bout the livestock, should we vacate this spot," drawled the cowboy, ably moving about with his hurts.

"No need to worry, son," said Wade. "we're onliest a few yards farther."

The trio made their way to the cabin in the clutch of the settlement, and were welcomed by all the rest.

"I'm right sorry to see you've been hit Missus Calhoon," said the cowboy, "I reckon I was a might careless, and let one get a little too close, but these ol' boys settled that issue."

"*Gracîas, señor, por de la interés,*" Rose replied, as she gratefully smiled to him.

"I ree-ly feel *muy büeno*, very well."

"Yeah, you were lucky," Bart agreed, "I'm happy we're all together. This is a large cabin, and there's plenty of room for us to be able to defend ourselves."

Harley spoke up, and exclaimed, "I'm near 'bout positive those Comanch' is the same bunch that was through this part of the country a couple of weeks ago. The Army was escortin' a payroll through to Amarillo, and stopped for a team exchange and said they'd re-exchange on their way back."

"They spotted these Injuns but they didn't have enough sojer-boys to spare to chouse 'em. They said it was Black Bull, a big, Comanch' shaman, and they'd send their troopers after 'em. Humph! They should'a hurried."

A white Indian pony with a painted red circle around its eye and three red stripes painted above both front knees, was running at top speed, urged by its feathered rider, toward the front of the cabin.

Bart saw him first, and then Lynx, as they both whirled to the front of the cabin and threw their pistol lead at the oncoming Comanche.

They both hit the man, and the horse shied at the close gunfire on its route to the cabin, whereupon it immediately dodged to the left. The force of those cartridges hitting the Indian and the sudden turn of his horse, caused the squalid tribesman to roll against the cabin door.

The Kwahadie was not dead, although struck twice with the gunfire from Bart and Lynx. The two shooters were not able to see the Indian from their gun ports unless they opened the door, for he was on the ground and lying up next to the door jamb.

The Indian remained stoic and silent while old man Parker could wait no longer and jerked the door inward to open it. Wade Parker could never accept the Comanche ways with their ruthless and barbaric acts toward their enemy. Their utter disregard for a human life was one of the primary causes for their actions.

Black Bull was particularly fond of disemboweling an enemy, handing him his own entrails, and watching a slow death he deemed pleasurable.

With the force of a bear and the quickness of a cat, Wade Parker reached for the Kwahadie Comanche and at the same time put his boot behind the knee, pulled the Indian's arm across his body, and flipped the man to his stomach.

Holding the Indian's head back by his hair, with his boot on his hips, he deftly and quickly reached under and slit open his throat.

"Not much reason to do that, Mister Parker," Bart exhorted. "I believe that Indian was a goner, and besides, we all don't exactly approve of your methods, especially the ladies."

"Well, sorry, ladies, but I do have my reasons."

Rosalita was comforting the suddenly nauseous Felicia Roberts, and Lynx decided to help his sidekick with the

Comanche's body, so they both grabbed his arms and dragged him away from the cabin and across the roadway leading into the settlement. They felt the ladies would be happier if they did.

Four of the arrows, among a dozen, found their mark in the back of old man Parker. One buried itself so deep, the tip projected through his sternum. He desperately tried to turn and pick up his fallen rifle, but collapsed and died in only seconds.

Lynx was hurriedly trying to take cover behind some fallen logs and brush beside the rutted roadway, as three Comanche warriors were racing their ponies toward him. He fired, and hit the lead rider.

Bart was anxiously watching the spot where the two men were down, and saw the arrows hit Wade Parker and watched the brave man fall and die. He and Doc Mullins then offered covering fire for Lynx from their positions inside the cabin. While this was taking place, another warrior group was forming for a raid against the cabin.

Doc Mullins swung clear around and started firing his shotgun at the red men riding in. Harley Henderson was right beside him and snapping off shots from his 1845, .44-.40, Colt revolver. On the first pass by, the Indians lost two more of their braves, shot from their ponies.

Bart bolted out the open door and raced to the fallen stage coach guard. He knew he was too late when he saw the pale death mask on the fatally wounded man.

Rosalita was watching her brave husband, and sucked in her breath when she saw what he obviously did not. Three of the Kwahadie braves, mounted in full run, were heading toward the gully where Bart was trying to lift the body of old man Parker, and bring him back inside.

Lynx hollered at the top of his lungs for Bart to leave the body and jump to the side of the logs where he'd gone. He was kneeling behind this deadfall and fired his rifle at the lead rider. His shot was wide, and the Comanche, in a full-feathered, medicine bonnet, swiped at Lynx as his horse jumped beside him. They both caught their arms in a lock and Lynx pulled with a quick jerk and managed to unseat the Comanche.

The second Indian was shot by the Texas cowboy, who was now standing in the open doorway of the cabin, firing his repeating rifle.

Felicia Roberts was not much help in assisting the men in the cabin, but Rosalita was outstanding in her judgement to help out. She was reloading weapons as quickly as the men would discard their arms, and opened cartridge boxes, and fetched water to each one, while all the time, trying not to let her husband see any sign of fear on her face.

Now, it was Bart who was in grave danger, away from the fortress of cover from the cabin, and in the throes of the hated Comanche, fighting for his life.

Lynx was battling a large, unusually strong, Indian. The red man had war paint on his face and on one arm, from his hand to his shoulder, and a grip of steel.

The third Indian of the trio, leaped from his horse with his war club in hand and ran toward Bart. This Comanche also was yelping in anticipation of a kill.

CHAPTER 7

Three companies of cavalry from Fort Sumner, New Mexico, were ordered over to Fort Stockton, Texas, a distance of about two hundred and seventy-five miles, and were scheduled to arrive in seven days.

The Army was expanding its forces in this portion of south Texas and drew from the fort in New Mexico since General Crook's two divisions were in western Arizona and eastern New Mexico. Captain Fitzgibbon was in charge. Three first and second Lieutenants comprised the officers, and each senior officer led a company of fifty-five men.

Unfortunately, for Lieutenant Roberts, he was not informed of the troop deployment in time to advise his wife, Felicia, that he would not be arriving in Portales to meet her.

In spite of the length of the journey, the cavalry companies were making a good time approaching their fifth day. It was certain they would bivouac this night at the way station in Kermit, Texas.

It was probably not more than five miles to the stage depot at Kermit, and Captain Fitzgibbon felt his command would arrive in the late afternoon. It was time to rest his troops and rest and water his horses before the final march into Fort Stockton.

Corporal Henson and trooper Parson, were riding fast from their mission as forward scouts, back to the Army column. They pulled rein at the head and were met by Captain Fitzgibbon and Lieutenant R.T. Roberts from A company.

"Report, Trooper," cried the captain. "Sir, it looks like a skirmish ahead at the stage way-station. 'Pears to be several dozen Indians there, circling the corral and cabins, and gunshots coming from the cabins. Parson's sure the Injuns are Comanche. We couldn't get close enough to ascertain any casualties, but it also 'pears that the corral had been set a-fire, and maybe one of the stage coach cabins in the assemblage, sir."

"Very, well, Corporal, a good report. Now Mister Roberts, take A company to the station, on the double. Prepare to engage the hostiles. We'll follow in reserve."

*   *   *

Bart intercepted the Comanche as he leapt through the air and wrestled him to the ground.The Indian was as strong as a bull, and managed to lock one of his legs behind Bart. He exerted enough force to flip him off to the side.

Bart Calhoon was a tall, fit man, who had been in his share of fights, but this was as tough as it had ever been for him because of the swiftness of move the Kwahadie used. He slashed with his long knife. Bart then countered with a step, a fake, and a powerful blow to the Indian's face with his forearm.

This move knocked the Indian to the side and Bart followed-up with another forceful punch to the Comanche's face.

Splat! Bart was certain he'd broken the Indian's nose. Blood flowed across the ochre and black war paint and the stringy mass was like a flowing river of spittle.

Bart couldn't locate his .44-.40 Colt and reached for his belted knife which he drew and plunged deep into the red chest of the startled Comanche. With a quick twist, he lifted the blade upward and back down, spilling out bowels. Bart backed away, and the Comanche, now on his knees, using both hands to try to hold his entrails inside, began the chant-singing of his medicine death song.

Meanwhile, Lynx was having a hard time with another Indian who delivered a blow with his war-club to the leg of Lynx. Now he was rising to stand over him, to render what could be a death chop, Bart had to act quickly.

He threw his body into the Indian with such force it carried them a few yards from the spot where Lynx was, and they rolled several times, each man trying to gain a favorable position.

The Comanche was formidable. His features were well defined; high cheekbones, not the wide face with a wide nose of the Apache. He had an aquiline nose like the beak of an eagle, a light, red-clay completion, with straight, black, un-cut hair. It was parted in the middle and braided on both sides of his neck.

He wore a bear-claw necklace around his throat and beaded, chamois-colored leggings with ornately- beaded moccasins.

"Tosi-Tivo, pa'nah'ah shik-ah, tek!"

The Comanche yelled as loudly as he could. Words directed only for the white-eyes."

The warrior faced his adversary, stoic and unflinching. His eyes could cut iron, and he made his way forward to battle.

Lynx had reloaded his Sharps rifle, but Bart was between him and the Comanche and it was irresponsible for him to fire a round.

As the Indian charged, he bent over and grabbed a handful of loose earth. He lifted his arm high in one direction, as a ploy, while he pitched the dirt in the eyes of Bart, who became his hated enemy.

Temporarily blinded, Bart brought his hands up to wipe the stinging, sandy dirt from his eyes, and the Comanche, at once, plunged his knife into the side of Bart, below his ribs.

Bart lost his balance, and tripped over some rocks, and fell, clutching his side. He saw his gun, lying beneath a sprig of pig-weed. He desperately needed to grab the weapon, but it was hopelessly beyond his reach. The Comanche was almost upon him with the speed of a cat.

In an instant, Lynx fired his rifle at the warrior who was, literally, in the air, leaping toward Bart. The force of the slug, as close as it was, actually pushed the Indian's body away from its intended goal.

Lynx fired a second time, and again, the third. The final shot hit the Indian full in the his throat, and blew away half of his neck.

Rosalita could not contain herself, for she had witnessed the entire escapade from the cabin window. She flew to Bart's side with an un-defined purpose.

Doc and Felicia were frantically calling to Rosalita when she darted out. She called to Bart as she reached his side.

"Amånte mia, ti' amo, Bart. Oh, my darling, *no muerté, no dado!"*

"It's all right, Rose, I'll be fine," Bart said.

"Quick," Lynx hollered to them both. "Get back in the cabin, afore any more of them varmints get to us. It'll be easier from inside."

CHAPTER 8

The survivors of the Comanche raid were inside the cabin, more secure in their numbers. Since there was a lull in the fighting, and no Indians seemed to be close by, the women began to prepare some food for everyone. The well was only a few steps from the rear of the cabin.

The cowboy asked Doc Mullins and the station master to cover him so he could attempt to water and feed the horses. He said his wound was not a hindrance.

The pot of beans that was steeping on the iron wood-stove, and the bread cakes from the pantry were served by Felicia, and Rosalita poured them all strong coffee. She was obvious-ly concerned with Bart's wound; it had started to bleed, again.

Doc Mullins finished his cup of coffee, and told Bart he wanted to redress his wound. Rosalita was helping him and noticed the jagged cut that was evident, The doctor assured her it would heal quickly.

Bart was more interested in consoling Lynx about the unfortunate death of his sidekick. They vowed to give ol' Wade a decent burial just as soon as this fight was over.

There was some question in their minds that they would prevail; however, it was a mater of time and the hope there were no more than the number of Comanches they'd figured on.

"Don't know what we'd a done 'th'out you, Doc," Harley said. "Good thing you got your medicine bag with ya, and all the stuff it takes for proper doctorin'."

"Obviously, I wasn't able to help old Mister Parker, God rest his soul, . . . but I'll be able to help you three. I do believe that cowboy's got snake blood in him," remarked the doctor, as he rose from the table and took his watch at the window. . . ."Here they come!" he shouted.

Bart rushed to the door and flung it open so he could fire at the Indians from the front, hoping this would give Walker Barnes some cover on his way back from the corral. "Hurry, son," he shouted to him. "You can start reloading now, Rose."

The Comanches were coming all right, they were riding for their lives, and not straight at the cabin area. In fact, they veered off at least a hundred yards before they reached the corral.

The men were firing their rifles at the red warriors as they were riding by, and Walker was kneeling behind a log at the corral, shooting his rifle. All at once he stood, and started to wave his arms over his head, with his hat in one hand.

Outside, Bart could hear the clear, familiar call of the Army bugler, blowing the charge. And then, at once, he could see what Wade saw. It was a company of soldiers, racing their mounts at full gallop, after the fleeing Indians, their sabers drawn, and ready for a combat duel with the Comanches.

The guide-on was carrying the flag with a big 'A' emblazoned on the half red and half white banner. The soldiers were all hollering and Bart detected a few of the Rebel yells among the federal troopers. "I counted eighteen Indians," Rosa exclaimed, as she and Felicia watched the spectacle.

It was not extremely difficult for the remaining band of Kwahadie warriors to out distance the structured charge of the soldiers. they split into groups of six and maneuvered through the sand-plated rocks with the grace and ease of deer. Lieutenant Roberts, leading the charge, raised his arm in a cease and desist motion, and drew a circle in the air for his men to reconnoiter. It took only a few minutes for A company to rein-in and re-form.

On their return ride back to Kermit station, The Lieutenant met the Captain and his guide-on, a Lieutenant Sawyer, from C company.

Lieutenant Curt McBride was holding D company at the old, Kermit station in reserve.

The soldiers had their orders to locate a camping ground for them to bivouac for the night, and the section detail was busy with this chore, about a quarter mile from the station.

Captain Fitzgibbon and his senior officers rode to the center of the establishment to meet with the civilians.

Doc Mullins and Bart Calhoon were the first two in the street where the officers dismounted, and the aides took their horses.

"Mighty glad to see you, Captain," the doctor said, and was reinforced by Bart, as they invited the men inside.

Captain Fitzgibbon introduced himself and his senior officers, as they stepped inside: "First Lieutenant, C. McBride, D company; First Lieutenant, F. Sawyer, C company, and First Lieutenant, R. Roberts of A comp . . ."

Felicia Roberts squealed with disbelief and cried out: "Robert, oh, Robby," as she interrupted, and ran to his side.

Caught unaware, the soldier was absolutely dumbfounded, but he managed to blurt out, "F-Felicia," and ardently wrapped his arms about her as she totally collapsed in his.

"Sir," he said to the captain, "Th-this is my wife. W-we were supposed to meet in Portales, but my orders changed, and I had no way of informing her that I would not be able to meet her stage coach."

Within a short time, everyone of the civilians were made comfortable, and the Army insisted in offering them an escort for their next day's departure to Lubbock.

Lynx was discussing the combat he and Bart had with the two Comanches, and his decision was that the big Indian was none other than the hated 'Black Bull.'

Captain Fitzgibbon related that at the staff meeting held at Fort Sumner, a copy of general orders was reviewed and he said that two platoons were dispatched to intercept the hostiles that were seen by the Army pay-wagon escort. It was obvious they failed to intercept them.

The next morning, the Army was ready to depart when a detail of eight troopers, including a grinning Lieutenant R.T. Roberts, came riding into the compound with the news that they'd been ordered to escort the stage to Lubbock.

Her clean-shaven husband told his wife, Felicia, that he'd been granted a ten day leave, starting the day they reached Lubbock.

The Saratoga, Texas cowboy, finished help- ing Lynx harness the six horses he needed to pull the coach. Bart was finished with his second cup of coffee, and said to Walker, "You can ride that bay mare I bought for my wife and wrangle my horse and the two extra coach horses, along side the stage. I'll be proud to spell you later."

Harley Henderson climbed up on the seat beside Lynx and said he'd ride shotgun for the company. He said they would most likely send someone else out to fix up the station buildings and corral at the Kermit way-station. He was "a-gonna rest for a couple weeks then take some time off." His grin was as big as his heart, when he stated this.

Bart, Rosalita, and Doc Mullins rode inside the coach, along with Felicia and her lieutenant husband. Of course, Sergeant Duffy was capable of commanding the assigned detail. The journey seemed rougher than expected, but all were pleased with their fate, and soon, all but Doc was asleep, inside.

CHAPTER 9

When the stage coach pulled into the livery stable grounds in Lubbock, the weather was changing for the worse. The escort of Army cavalry reined up outside the stables and dismounted and assembled nearby. Lieutenant Roberts rode the last five miles into Lubbock with his detail of troopers.

One of the tasks the soldiers helped with was the removal of the tarpaulin-covered body of old man Parker from off the top of the coach. It was decided that Parker's body should be taken to his home, for proper burial.

Bart and the Lieutenant were busy discussing their respective plans concerning a two night stay-over, since the stage for Amarillo wasn't due to depart until the day after tomorrow.

"The troopers will start for Fort Stockton first thing in the morning," the officer said, to Bart. "I think Felicity and I shall stay here for several days and then get the a stage for Fort Stockton, too."

"So, you'll be spendin' a few days of your leave-time here, Lieutenant? Why are you in such a hurry to get to Fort Stockton?"

"Ironically, my wife's family moved within forty miles of there from Saint Louis, Missouri. Felicia's father is with the S.P. railroad, so it really is a break for me to be assigned into Fort Stockton," he replied.

"Rosa and I are headed for Hartley county, and my folks' ranch near the Rita Blanca river. been two years since I've seen 'em, and they're going to meet my new bride for the first time."

Rosalita and Felicity came from the empty stage coach and each took the arm of the men they adored. The couples decided they would meet again for supper in the hotel, and turned to unpack and freshen up.

The stage coach company representative and the sheriff wanted to speak with the passengers, and Doc Mullins wanted to check on the healing wound of Rosalita and the hip-point wound of Bart, as an early evening wind whistled it's chilly sermon of the events to come.

"Oh, Bart, I am so hoppy for us to finally be alone again," she cooed, her dark eyes flashing the admiration she had for her new husband.

"You're right, sweetheart. You've been through an awful lot these past days and it will be good for us to get to the ranch. I'm so anxious for you to meet my ma'am and my daddy. We'll have to make a decision about returning to Presidio, and my job at the mill," Bark exclaimed.

The thunder was enormously loud, and sounded as though it came from the street below their hotel window. The temperature must have dropped over twenty-five degrees, and there was no question of a hard storm forcing its way through the district.

"I think I'll close the window the rest of the way, and turn down the lamp," Bart remarked, as he crossed the room.

When he turned, he was startled at first at what he witnessed. Rosa had completely divested herself of her clothing, and was lying on the bed sheets with her arms outstretched, beckoning her *amante* to spend himself within her ample wares.

Carefully, and hurriedly, Bart took off his boots, he undid his shirt and removed it and stepped out of his britches, which he left, with all the rest of his clothing, on the floor. The wind as whistling its eerie songs and the rain it brought in was cascading from the eaves of the hotel roof, and pounding, drum-like, against the window.

The softness of her skin and the gentle acceptance of his parted lips on her firm breasts, was a consummate sign of mutual ecstasy for them both.

She was concerned about the wound Bart suffered in his side, and he was fretful of the soreness in her arm, as they cautiously moved to gain comfort for one another. They giggled when they both denied any discomfort from any ongoing action.

"Matr^monio es muy bien, amånte mia, y ti amo, y yo muy agrdecîdo." Rosalita whispered these words to her *vaquero*, as he was making ardent love with her.

"You are so beautiful," Bart sternly told her, when he lay back, momentarily, to visualize her loveliness . . .again.

The snow that fell during the night had drifted crisp and pristine in front of the hotel, when Bart and Rosa awakened to prepare for their continuing journey.

It became increasingly more difficult for his wife to raise herself from the warm comfort of the bed, and untangle herself from th embrace she kept with Bart.

"Tengo muy frio, enamorå mia," she spoke to Bart , who arose and began searching the luggage for some warmer clothing.

"I'm afraid you're just going to have to get out of bed and get dressed, my love. Here, put on this extra lindsey shirt, and wrap up with that serape," he laughingly said to his beautiful, sleepy-headed wife.

"Oh, alma, I do love you."

It became another hour or so before they both presented themselves downstairs in the hotel dining room for breakfast.

No sooner than they were seated, a demure Felicia, and her handsome officer husband appeared in the entry, and were asked to join the Calhoons' for breakfast. Felicity and Rosa greeted each other with a hug, blushing faces, and girlish giggles.

Outside, the town was awake and lively with merchants sweeping all their entry-ways and board-walks. A freight wagon was being loaded and the team was blowing steam from their nostrils, while awaiting their departure.

The barber and the banker exchanged greetings, and remarked about the first snowfall, as together, they entered the coffee house. Several drovers rode into town and tied their wet ponies to the one hitching rail in front of the dram house.

Lynx Walters strode into the dining room at the hotel where the Calhoons and the Roberts were still enjoying their breakfast.

"Good morning, all," he said. "In about an hour and a half the stage to Amarillo will be ready to go, and I'm fixin' to drive this one, too."

"Who's ridin' shotgun for you, this trip, Lynx?" Bart wanted to know.

"That west-Texas cowboy . . ."

"You mean, Walker Barnes?"

"Yeah, I do. Said he decided to go on to Amarillo, after he telegraphed his boss, yesterday. So, he said he'd just hire on for this ride as my sidekick. I know I'll miss old man Parker, but I'm proud to have Walker along."

The snow was falling with more authority as the morning progressed, and the passengers for the stage were assembled in the hotel lobby, awaiting some late decision to postpone the departure.

The two children were sitting on the divan in the hotel lobby, while their mother was settling their account at the front desk. The little girl answered she was seven years old, and told Rosa that her big brother had just turned nine, and they were traveling to Amarillo to visit their grandparents, thank you.

The children seemed as they were dressed warm enough, with woolen coats and scarves and rabbit-skinned gloves. She had a hand-knitted cap covering all but the ends of her curls, and he proudly wore the mark of every Texas kid, a felt, wide-brimmed, cowboy hat. They were both well-behaved and polite, stoic but still managed a coy and shy smile.

"I'm very grateful to you, Mister Potter, for waking us early enough to get ourselves ready to leave for Amarillo today, instead of tomorrow, as planned," the children's mother said to the old hostler, as she checked out.

"You're welcome, Missus Crawford. I guess it was Mister Carrington's decision to leave a day early, after all, it is his company, and his animals and stage coaches. I understand he must get to Amarillo on urgent business, whether it's snowing' or not."

"All right, children, you must both attend to your morning toilet, and do it now. We're going to get on the stage in about fifteen minutes. "Tombo," she said to the little boy," you go with Mister Potter, and Annie, you may come with me. Hurry, now," she gently spoke.

Rosalita was astounded at the two youngsters' manners, as well as their attentiveness to their mother. She was certain these children were being reared with deportment and devotion, and in a fleeting second, thought to herself, "now that's the way ours will turn out to be."

CHAPTER 10

Walker was helping Lynx load the luggage in the huge canvas sling at the rear of the coach. Once again, Bart tied both his haltered horses to the back end of the stage and lashed both saddles on top.

Martin Carrington was already inside the coach anxiously awaiting the rest of the passengers to board. Bart gave his hand to assist Missus Crawford on the step, and turned and lifted little Annie to her mother. Tombo grinned, and climbed the step and entered by himself.

The wet snow was starting to add to itself, and sticking to the flat surfaces including the tarpaulin covering the luggage and saddles. Rosa was bidding a fond farewell to her friend, Felicia, and exchanged last minute hugs with her and Lieutenant Roberts.

"Time to board, 'alma,' said Bart, as he helped his olive-skinned beautiful wife into her inside seat. Lynx gathered the reins as Walker waved his goodbye.

"How long ya reckon it'll take us to get to Cory station, Lynx?" The Texas cowboy inquired.

"Don't rightly know, Walker, this snow just ain't lettin' up, a'tall. It's got to be better for us to head west on the Clovis road, and stop at the Yellow House river station. Clem

Archer'll have enough room to put everyone up for a bed, and he has a good supply pen of remuda horses, too."

"You believe that'll cost us a 'xtry day, a-goin' that way, pard?"

"Might, but this snow's too powerful for us to make any time headin' north. I reckon Mister Carrington'll just have to put up with the delays. Never counted on this much snow, least this early in the year."

The six horses were in good shape, and pulling well, but Lynx was not trying to hurry them. He knew that with a good nights rest and some extra grain, they would do for the trip, without changing.

Lynx wheeled the teams into the Yellow House river stage station, and before he started to unhitch, he jumped down and called inside for Clem Archer.

Martin Carrington nearly fell from the coach when he jumped out, furious with Lynx.

"What th' hell's going on, anyway? This isn't the Cory station, Walters?"

"That's right, Mister Carrington, it just wasn't in the cards for us to try to reach Cory. We most likely would've not made it through the Piñion-Pine pass, or ever got over Cotton creek in this storm, Mister Carrington. You pay me to drive this stage and my responsibilities also include the safety of the passengers. Now, ain't that what's on your newspaper and poster advertisin', MISTER Carrington?"

Walker Barnes watched, slack-jawed, as Carrington spun around and headed for the station and its roaring fireplace.

"You got some cold blood in you, too. ain't cha, Lynx? Ain't that the man what signs them payroll checks?" Walker was grinning from ear to ear, awaiting an answer from the grizzled coach driver.

"He'll get over it. I been workin' for the company since he started it, and he don't pay enough to hire someone new."

Bart unhitched his two saddle horses from the rear of the coach, and took them toward the lean-to at the corral, to feed.

Clem Archer was already helping Lynx unhitch the six-up, and Walker was unloading the luggage. "Just set it by the side of that big room," Clem's wife said, to the cowboy. "I intend to have supper for everybody in 'bout a half hour, meantime, I'll show you where your rooms are."

Rosalita was helping Walker with all the luggage, and she put hers and Barts' in one of the rooms, then came out to help Ruby Crawford and her children.

"Don't touch that black valise!" Martin Carrington shouted to the cowboy and to Rosa, who looked up in shock.

"I'll handle that bag myself," he said, "now, which is my room?"

"In that large room on the end. You should be comfortable there with your two employees, Mister Carrington," stated the station master's wife.

"Not acceptable," he shouted, again. "In my position, I need a room alone."

Bart entered the station lodge just as the stage coach company owner was shaking his finger at the manager's wife.

"Whoa-up, there, Mister Carrington, we need to correct this right now."

"N-never mind," he replied, "I was just upset about the route change. It-it will be fine - uh, this room will be just fine . . . uh, excuse me, . . . uh, everyone." Carrington picked up the black valise and clutching it to his bosom, retreated to the large room, slamming the door.

Rosalita quickly sidled up to Bart and clutched his arm. She looked up into his eyes with a quizzical expression, as if to question him on his outburst.

"Forget it, *alma, mia*," he smiled, which is our room? I need a clean shirt."

Walker Barnes entered next, and was followed by Lynx and Clem. They all had stomped the snow from their boots, and shook the mantle of snow from their coats, before pegging them behind the door.

"That fire shore feels mighty nice," the Texas cowboy remarked, as he poked at the large, mesquite logs spewing heat and aroma.

Tombo, and his little sister, Annie, peeked out from their room door before they both approached the warm fireplace, and sat in front, cross legged, on a woven Indian rug.

"Bet you young-uns are hungry," Lynx said to both. "It won't be too long, now."

Their mother appeared; she having changed to a more casual attire of men's trousers and a woolen shirt, fitting snug on a handsome, tall and stately figure.

Walker and Lynx bumped into each other when they stood up, simultaneously, as Ruby Crawford entered the room.

Rosa was helping Missus Archer with the supper which was about to be set on the long table, and smiled as she crossed the room to call Bart and Mister Carrington to be seated. The children sat on each side of their mother, and Lynx and Walker sat next to them.

Clem, as usual, sat at the head of the table and the seats for Bart and Rosa as well as Martin Carrington, were on the opposite side. Clem's wife sat down at the foot of the table, while Clem gave thanks for everyone's health and safety.

With the final 'a-men', Carrington made his appearance and immediately sat at the open chair, assuming it was his.

"All right, folks, let's begin. If you'll pass the chicken, Missus Calhoon, and help yourself, I'd be obliged," Clem stated. "It's all right if you wanted to give them starvin' young-uns somethin' first," he winked at the children.

"Just pass it around the table, dear, there's plenty more to come," the station manager's wife spoke to Rosalita.

After everyone had their servings, the conversation began in earnest concerning the state of affairs to soon occur.

Lynx spoke up first. "The snow was just getting worse on the east trail to Amarillo, and that's the reason we drove west to your station, Clem. I want everyone to understand that we may have to hole-up here, at least as long as the snow falls."

"Hopefully, it'll let up some when the winds take it more south-east," stated Walker, "and it warms up a might."

CHAPTER 11

More than a foot of snow lay on the ground and greeted Clem as he dutifully made his way to the corral and shed where the livestock were waiting to be fed.

"I reckon I can bust that film of ice from the water troughs, Mister Archer," said the cowboy, stepping in the same tracks, while following him to the shed.

"Stopped snowin', Walker. I 'magine Martin Carrington will insist on starting for Amarillo today. Yonder comes Lynx, we should get his decision, though."

The three teamsters discussed the possibilities of the stage leaving today, and decided they could start soon after a breakfast was prepared and consumed.

"You just make an invoice out to the Carrington Brothers Stage and Transport company, for the food and lodging for our group, Clem. I'll sign it and take it to the Amarillo office, with us. Be sure to add the horse feed too," Lynx added.

"Oh, oh, Bart," Rosa whispered, from her place nestled next to her amorous husband. *"Yo tengo que irmé, alma mia, con permîso,* Chu must let me go, that I can help the *señora con la comida,* uh, with the foods. It is become too lates for us to start with the foolishness now. Ees time for *desayüno."*

Bart was laughing at his olive-skinned beauty, when he pulled her back with his sinewy arms to the comfort of the bed.

"I must go, with your permission, to help fix the breakfast," he mocked her words she spoke to him in Spanish, and he just laughed louder this time, at her futile attempt to break from his grasp.

"Oh, all right, *amanté mia,* but I am *muy timîdo* to appear by myself. We will make love, and then, we will go out together."

"This is very special," he exclaimed. The morning sunlight that reflects off the snow-covered roofs of those out buildings is dancing with the light that comes in that bedroom window over there. You know, it brightens your eyes, and tells me you have found some happiness." Her husband was holding her closer with each word he spoke.

Breakfast was over and it was time for the group to resume their journey. Even though it had stopped snowing, the road would be covered, and the trip would take a bit longer.

Lynx was just as much interested in starting as Martin Carrington was. He felt the sooner he could get this coach to Amarillo, the sooner he would be rid of Carrington's wrath.

Bart, once again, tied his grulla gelding and the bay mare of Rosas', to the rear of the stage coach, and packed the saddles on top. Everyone was saying their goodbyes' to the Archers, and were very grateful for their hospitality.

Walker Barnes asked Tombo's mother if she'd allow the boy to ride with him, on top, but Martin Carrington would not allow it, and gruffly told the boy to set back down and be quiet.

"I didn't hear the lad speak a word," Bart addressed the stage owner. "If that is your policy, so be it, but don't you be taking out any of your frustrations on the boy, after all, as we all are, he's a paying customer to your company."

The driver reached the Littlefield pass and turned his six horses onto the trail directly north, leading on to their first stop at Sunnyside, on the Running Water river.

Inside the stage, the passengers were adjusting to the cold weather. Two large, wool, Indian blankets covered the ladies legs, and little Annie and her brother were sharing the one with their mother. The canvas side flaps had been drawn over the windows to keep out as much air as possible, of course, this rendered any outside vision, rather difficult. Ten more miles passed when the stage arrived at the swollen, muddy banks of the Blackwater river, which had to be forded if they were to continue onward to Sunnyside.

The children and their mother were asleep, and Bart removed his arm from around Rosa's shoulder, and slightly opened the canvas window cover on the side next to where he was seated.

"What'chu see, my hosban'?" Rosa asked him. Eet stopped snowing, yes?"

The cowboy, riding shotgun, saw them about the same time Bart saw them, from his view inside the coach. It had not, in fact, stopped snowing, rather, it was snowing harder at the moment Lynx had the three-team hitch halted.

Two wagons were hitched with a team to each wagon, and each one resting hip-shot.

At least four Indian ponies were tied to slender cottonwood trees near the bank of the Blackwater river. A gray, canvas tent was set-up about thirty yards away, and two small fires were burning, side by side in front of the tent. Bart counted five Indians and two men that did not appear to be Indian. The roaring noise the running river caused, and the muffled sound of the coach approaching down wind in the snow, most likely caught the party of seven off guard.

Bart warned the passengers inside to be alert and to keep quiet. He said he and Lynx and Walker would find out who and how they happened to be here, too.

Bart climbed down from the coach and the cowboy climbed down from his perch.

The Indian squatting behind the cook fire remained there, while two Indians moved beside one of the two wagons. One man, dressed in a buffalo robe coat, and cradling a rifle, walked toward the stage and extended his hand upward, palm out, in the traditional sign of peace. He wore a wolf-pelt cap and had a long, dark beard.

"You folks is off'n yore trail jes a bit, ain't ye? This creek's swole-up and not passable, anyways, friend. Whar ye headed to in this weather?" He asked.

Bart eyed the stranger cautiously, and noted Lynx had secured the reins and had the shotgun across his lap, still in his drivers seat aboard the stagecoach.

Walker appeared about ten paces to the right side of the coach, and he was watching the two Indians that went to the wagon loaded with something under a heavy canvas cover. This particular wagon seemed to be heavy with load, and siting deep in the snow covered ground.

The other wagon, only yards away, did appear to be empty, and uncovered.

The overcast day offered only a dim light. "We're on our way to Amarillo, by way of the Sunnyside station at the Running Water river," Bart answered. "I reckon the river's too high to cross just now, so we'll have to wait it out or find a long detour. We had to detour from east of here, yesterday, so I 'spose it makes little difference. What brings you here?"

By this time the second white man was approaching the stage. He was armed, but his pistol was holstered. A seemly grin crossed his face as he spoke.

"I figure you folks just better turn that there stage around, and go back the way you came. We ain't got 'nuf vittles to feed you if you was to try campin' here this evenin'."

"Sorry, neighbor," Lynx shouted from his position atop the stage seat. "These teams are gonna need some rest, and we'll just stay here 'til that river be crossable."

Not heeding Bart's advise to remain inside the coach and keep quiet, Martin Carrington stepped from the coach and demanded to know what the discussions were about, and what everyone planned to do immediately.

CHAPTER 12

Unnoticed, one Indian at the loaded wagon untied the tether that held the team, while the other Indian turned and unloosened the four, spotted ponies tied to the cottonwood saplings. The one who untied the team climbed aboard the wagon and shouted at the horses to pull away.

Buffalo-robe turned and yelled at the Indian driving the wagon to stop.

"Hey, you red bastard, bring that wagon back . . . we ain't got our money yet."

The Indian that was crouched by the cook fire rose, and as quick as a coon skinning a fish, had his bow flexed, and fired one arrow deep in the back of the second man, then followed with another arrow.

The other Indians had already made their quick steps to the horses, and vaulted to their backs. one stopped with a spare horse for the red man who'd just shot the arrows.

Bart dropped to one knee, and then drew his pistol to fire at the fleeing red men. One brave circled behind the stage, and let a barrage of arrows fly toward the cowboy, on the right.

A second Indian rode in with a hideous whoop, and plunged his lance into Buffalo-Robe, pinning him to the cold, snowy ground. Bart fired once and slew the warrior as he turned.

Lynx let both barrels of his shotgun do his talking. It spoke to an Indian ready to shoot an arrow into the belly of Carrington, and blew him off his pony, that also felt some of the shots.

Walker Barnes ran to the coach to make certain the children were hidden as best as possible, and that everyone kept down. Rosalita and the children's mother were lying atop the blankets that covered both the children.

Buffalo-robe was bent over himself in the snow, and coughing blood from the lance penetration, slowly dying. His cohort was already dead, the arrows came into his back and pierced his sternum. It was overt to Bart that three of the Indians were making good their escape. One in the wagon, and two horseback. Lynx caught the wounded, standing pony. It belonged to a Kiowa!

"Look at this, Calhoon," Lynx said. "This pony has the Kiowa shield tied to its girth rope. Seems to me that they're a long way from their territory. They must be making big medicine with the Comanch', near-by. I wonder what they're a-doin' this far south?"

Bart rushed to the stage to check on Rosa and Ruby Crawford and her children. Walker Barnes was reloading his pistol and told Bart they were all safe and sound.

"Are they gone, my hosban'?" Rosa asked Bart, as she emerged from the coach and proceeded toward the men lying in the snow. Ruby was trying to keep Tombo inside the coach with his sister, but he managed to crawl out the other door and make his way over to Walker.

Lynx was explaining the scenario to Bart and the cowboy, while Carrington was inspecting the blood, cold bodies of the two, dead white men.

"Boys, it looks like we interrupted a fancy pow-wow here, this afternoon. I'm certain these bozos were selling rifles to these Indians, and we busted in 'fore they was finished. Didja hear Buffalo-robe?"

"Why y'all reckon them Keeowa boys didn't fire any o'them raffles? Walker inquired.

"I don't think the Indians knew how to operate them," Bart answered. "I reckon they were going to tell them after the Indians paid 'em for the guns. The Kiowas likely had money gathered from raids on ranches and from wagon train raids, over the months."

"Well," Lynx stated, "we should be able to ford that river pretty soon. If that snow can make up its mind to stop, the water will go down some more. I think it's rocky enough for a fairly solid base and those teams can make it if you and Walker each throw ropes on both sides of the stage, from your saddle horses, Bart."

"Oh, my God!" cried Carrington. "I know this man . . . h-he's my bookkeeper from the Clovis office. It's Amos Sutton! Where did he get money to buy guns to resell?"

The men worked hard for the next several hours to cut some timber to lash to the sides of the empty wagon, in order to be able to float it across the river in case the water proved to be too deep.

Walker said he would drive the wagon across first and unhitch the team. The cowboy took one of the horses to swim the river back to help with the stage. Carrington stayed inside the coach with Missus Crawford and her children, as Lynx shouted to the team. Rosalita rode her bay mare across, and had very little difficulty with the swim. Bart and Walker managed to affix guide ropes on the coach and helped steady it through the river.

The two bodies were wrapped in one of the tarpaulins and placed in the wagon that Walker took across first. Now, he hitched the horse he used, back to the wagon, which he would drive to the Sunnyside station.

It finally stopped snowing later in the afternoon, and when they reached the opposite shore, they decided to wait until arriving at the station to celebrate.

It was suppertime when Lynx pulled the stage coach into the way station at Sunnyside, and surprisingly, there had been less than a trace of collected snow at the station. Augustus Kappler, with his wife, Marta, were the station owners, and heartily welcomed the unexpected guests.

"Ja, ja. You vill yust shtay here dis nicht, und Marta vill feed efferwun." 'Gus' was helping unhitch and put up the livestock that came along with the stage, and remarked about the spotted pony that was following the other horses.

"Figure it's Kiowa, Gus," Lynx remarked. He began telling him the story of their strange encounter at the Blackwater river.

"We're on our way to Amarillo, if this weather will ever cooperate," Bart said to the station master. "How long do you think it will take us to travel there?"

"Vell, dot's a goot kvestion, ja. It iss about turdy-five miles to Hereford, und anudder forty-five miles from dere to Amarillo. You leaf in der mornink und you get dere der followink day, ja." August Kappler was a huge person with large forearms and a kind soul, and a big heart to match his enthusiasm.

Supper was over and Ruby Crawford was busy putting her children in bed to sleep. She would share their bed with them later, but for now she was going to help Rosa and Marta with the supper dishes.

The men were enjoying their smoking in front of the roaring fire in the big, main room in the station. Except for Carrington. He'd already retired with his ever present, and constantly carried, black valise.

Perhaps thirty minutes had passed when Bart suddenly rose from his chair and went toward the front window.

"Someone's out there, Gus," Bart said, "in fact, sounds like quite a few."

Walker jumped up toward the kitchen and Lynx and Gus rushed to the doorway.

The knock at the door that Gus answered, brought forth the high sheriff from Curry county, New Mexico, where Clovis was the county seat.

Bart saw from the window, about a dozen men, All heavily armed, in front of the station, all formed up in a posse.

CHAPTER 13

"Sorry to disturb you this evenin'. I'm Sheriff Towne, and my posse and I left Clovis this morning, on the trail of two outlaws tracked this direction."

"We might have a lot to talk about, Sheriff." Bart exclaimed, as he motioned for Lynx and Walker to follow him outside.

After viewing the bodies, still in the unhitched , empty wagon in the barn, the sheriff and his deputy confirmed the men were the ones that were wanted.

The two, Amos Sutton and 'Buffalo' Frank McCormack, were positively identified by the deputy who had the wanted posters.

The sheriff was interested in the story of what had happened at the Blackwater river. He had not been aware that the Kiowa and Comanche were together in a plot to buy firearms. He did tell Bart that McCormack, and an Army deserter, got into one of the sub-arsenals at Clovis and confiscated two hundred, M1849 rifles.

Martin Carrington was visibly shaken when Bart awakened him to tell of the findings of he New Mexico sheriff. The sheriff wanted to question Carrington about his employee, Amos Sutton.

"H-he's been with our company since we started back in '69. I hired him from a teller's job at the Pioneer bank in El Paso, and moved him to Clovis, later."

"Sutton," said the sheriff, "was kin to this McCormick feller, and when that Army deserter was caught later, McCormack hunted up Sutton to help him out."

"I guess Sutton figured he'd supplement his income by entering into this business with his cousin." The sheriff was still trying to figure how they were able to contact the Indians about them buying firearms; and would they be in a position to follow with more later on?

"Wary vell, Sheriff," spoke Augustus, "you boiss vill take, I guess, der vagon und der team, dat belonks to dem crooks, und der bodies vill keep in dis vedder ontil you get to Clovis, ja?" Martin Carrington, now hurried back inside.

The posse decided to leave at once for Clovis. It meant a lot shorter trail time, and there would be reward money to share among them, plus the pay they would receive from the county tax payers, for forming the posse.

The Army was going to have to be informed of the situation of the two hundred rifles that made off with the band of red men of the Kiowa-Comanche nations. Bart said the Indian Agency people should be questioned and he felt they would know exactly with which of the chiefs they should pow-wow.

Morning at the Sunnyside station woke with a clearing sky, and no sign of any more snow. In fact, the temperature warmed with a respectable restraint.

Rosalita crept from her bed warmth and drew the room shade before she climbed back beside her husband. Her heart was filled with happiness, as she listened to Bart's clear, controlled breathing, as he slept soundly next to her warm body.

She gently kissed his handsome face, and spoke his name, ever so quietly, into his ear.

"Oh, Bart-Bart, I love chu so very much."

The stage pulled away from Sunnyside immediately after breakfast and started for the station at Hereford, Texas. The spotted pony had sufficiently healed and was very well broken to ride. He was gelded, and had a good disposition. Walker offered to shoe the pony when they got to Hereford, but Lynx warned him that it may be an arduous task, betting it had never been shod.

Inside the coach, Little Annie sat as her mother was reading her Edgar A. Guest's, a 'Child's Garden of Verses'. Tombo heard, although pretending he did not, as he kept his vigil out the side window of the stage coach.

The lad was suddenly rewarded, for in the part of the country they were now passing, the landscape was deciduous with trees shedding. This offered an unobstructed view of wild game abounding here. East of the coach grazed large herds of buffalo.

On top, where Walker was seated, he too, was watching the lava flow of shaggy, black bodies, swarming over the semi-crystal light reflecting from the dusting of snow on the cinnamom-colored, long, range grasses.

He pointed them out to Lynx before leaning down to inform the passengers, but Tombo had already alerted them.

These were the first bison that Rosa had ever seen, and she was fascinated at the sight.

Little Annie was holding her nose, until her mother corrected the unladylike appearance she projected.

The daylight was delightful, as it presented a sunny, clear aura, even with a slight chill in the air. Perhaps the snow was truly over, which should please the passengers, as well as the drivers - not to mention, the horses.

It was time to pull rein, and make a stop to rest the teams. Lynx headed off the roadway to where some cottonwoods were offering some shade, beside a tiny stream.

The large, wicker basket that Marta Kappler filled with chicken and other sandwiches, were a welcome sight for all who decided they were hungry for some lunch.

Walker quickly had a small coffee-fire started, doing so after he'd helped Lynx unhitch the coach teams. Bart untethered the three horses that were tied to the back of the coach, and took them to the small stream, to water.

Lynx did the same with his six horses, and decided they would spend less than an hour at this repose, before heading onward to the Hereford way station.

Ruby Crawford was talking with with Rosa while the children were playing beside the stream, and Lynx was sheltered on the ground beneath a tree where he propped his head, for a quick snooze.

"Wonder why that Carrington feller stays to hisself so much of the time? Walker related to Bart, pointing to the stage company owner.

"It's a mystery to me, pard. It almost seems as though he has something to hide, or else he's just naturally a sort of a loner."

"I'd like to know what's so all-fired important in that black valise of his'n," Walker said. "Some time I'm a gonna ask him."

"Oh, no - no!," cried out Martin Carrington, from inside the coach. "It's Indians! And they're headed here, toward us."

Walker raced to the stream and gathered up Annie and Tombo in one swoop of his arms. He ran back to the coach with them, and proceeded to help Lynx get the teams hitched back together again.

Bart made certain Rosalita and Ruby were also in the coach, and caught the saddle horses to tie to the back. He tied the Indian pony alongside the stage, and just outside the window, with a long lead rope. This done, he finished helping with the coach horses.

Carrington was still inside, and he was fumbling with a revolver he retrieved from his black valise. Within only moments, the men had the stage coach all ready to travel. They decided to stay on the roadway leading to the Hereford depot.

The Indians were still about a mile from the stage, but their horses weren't in a full run. Lynx hollered that the coach horses would be able to stay ahead for quite some time, and not to waste any shells.

A sudden thought occurred to Bart, as he double checked his Spencer repeating rifle, and the two pistols he kept holstered. He was certain these Indians were hostile, but what if they were outfitted with the rifles that were taken at the Blackwater river? He reached over and gently touched Rosalita, and exclaimed, "Everything is going to be fine."

Young Tombo wasn't frightened, at least, he certainly didn't show it. He was probably more excited just watching the Indians.

"Do think they're going hunting after those buffalo we saw, Mother?" he asked, not dreaming they may be in peril.

"Hush, darling, just keep down, and allow the men here to handle matters," his mother answered him.

"Faster, driver," Carrington screamed out the stage coach window. "Go faster!!"

"How many they are, *amanté mia?*" Rosa questioned her husband.

"Not sure, alma," he replied. "They still are a good ways away. Looks like a dozen or so. Now, don't worry."

CHAPTER 14

The stagecoach was still about eighteen miles from the next station, situated about a half-mile south of the settlement of Hereford. Lynx had the team steadied out and not racing, but never the less, still at a fast pace.

The prairie in this area was starting to rise in altitude, and there was some rolling hills cropping up in the distance. This meant the road had to make some turns on occasions, to dodge some outcrops of rocky hills and a few trees.

It was apparent by now that the Indians had spotted the stage. The band turned north from their easterly direction, and came at them fast.

Strangely, there was no rifle fire from the ensuing warriors, only yelling. Was it possible, Bart wondered to himself, that these Indians were indeed, a hunting party in search of the buffalo, and stumbled on this coach by mistake? Were they Comanche? Kiowa? Were they really a hostile band?

Lynx was heading the coach horses toward the sand hills that were appearing a short distance away, and shouting loudly at his horses now, to run fast for the boulders at the first one of those hills.

The stage stopped inside the confine of several rises and creeped closer to the side of a larger mesa where there were many more larger boulders. Bart told them all to get out and take cover behind any of the big rocks. Walker Barnes was already hurrying to get in a forward, protective position.

Lynx set the coach brakes, and then wrapped the reins around the long handle, before he took his place, rifle in hand, across from the cowboy. Bart stayed with Rosa, Ruby, and her children, and directed Carrington to take some cover below and in front of them.

The Indians were nearing the area where the coach had turned into the rock-covered hills, and pulled-up short, out of gun-shot range. Here, they split, about half riding up the far side of the hill, and the rest, covering what could prove to be, a lane of escape.

Another dangerous situation was occurring in the travelers' lives, and Bart knew how serious this could turn out, but was determined to not let anyone know.

There was no rifle fire, and the men knew the Indians were without the dreaded rifles they were certain had fallen into the redskins hands.

The insatiable band of Indians who held the front side of the rock-strewn pass were capable, however, of simply waiting out the patience of their enemy.

Five of the eleven red men who had split, made their way to the back side of the small mesas where the two ladies and the two children were hiding behind the rock cover. These five also split-up. Two were silently approaching the rear of the hiding place of the Crawford children.The other three Indians took a flank movement around the side of a large rock where Bart was stationed, crouched be-hind boulders, and began firing arrows at the group. One of the three continued on down the hill toward Martin Carrington.

Bart raised himself slightly for an unabated shot from his Sharps rifle, at the closest Indian. The crack of the rifle sent the cartridge into the middle of the brave's chest, and spilled him from his hillside cover. He tumbled forward, rolled twice, and died while still bleeding.

During this exchange, one of the Indians, behind the children, brazenly stood and shot a cedar-shafted, flint-headed arrow, deep into the back of Ruby Crawford's spine, denying her any further life.

The second of the two Indians raced toward the children, and with his bow, smacked at Rosa, causing her to fall.

"Bart!" she screamed. "Bart! Oh, hurry. The Indian grabbed the two little children, and sped back up the incline of the mesa, where his pony was tethered,

Bart could only see a portion of what was happening. He knew he killed the one Indian, but he couldn't locate the other two. He instantly ran as fast as he could, the seventy-five yards up the hill from where he'd heard Rosalita call. He arrived to see Ruby dead in Rosa's arms.

"Rosa, are you all right, are you hit?"

"No, my hosban'. The *niños,*" she screamed, "he took the children, oh! oh! Bart, their mama *es muérto,* She ees dead, Bart, and they have the children." Bart hastened his pursuit.

As he started after the children, he hesitated and hollered down to where Lynx and Walker were, near the front of the pass, and maybe another seventy-five yards.

"Up here," he shouted. "Hurry, up here," he repeated. "Lynx, Walker, can you see me? Can you hear me?" he was waving his arms, and motioning for them to come where he was.

Walker heard him and came running. Lynx left his position across the road, and made his way toward the coach and the saddle horses. He had yet to see any Indians coming from where they originally separated.

When Walker reached the spot on the hill where Bart was, he was told of the dreadfulness of the occasion, and

Bart asked him to look after Rosalita, then he ran back down the hill to retrieve his horse.

"Walker's with my wife," Bart told Lynx. He explained everything, while saddling his grulla. "There's two Injuns still on the side of the hill, near to where Carrington's hiding. He's well armed, I hope he's a good shot. You best stay with the coach, and watch the front way into this pass. I'm goin' after those kids."

Suddenly, three rifle shots were heard from where Carrington was, followed a second or two later, by one more shot.

Bart was mounted now, and started up the side of the mesa to where he heard the shots. Not three hundred yards from the spot, Bart saw two dead Indians within ten feet of each other, in line with Carrington's shots. As Bart rode on farther, he saw Carrington wave and then stand up. His valise was in his hand and in it there was stuck an arrow shaft.

Bart asked Carrington to start for the coach and help Lynx watch the front. He said he had a job to do, and Lynx would fill him in on what had just happened. Then he turned and said, "Good job, Mister Carrington."

The grulla that Bart rode was a blue-gray, mouse-color, in the Dun horse family. Dark mane and tail, dark legs, and muscular with a good disposition. To say it was far superior to the smaller, more feral, Indian ponies, with shorter legs, and unable to run as fast, was a pronounced understatement.

Bart had only a thought of how many Indians were involved with this raid, but he knew for certain, three were dead. His wife had said there were two that took the children, and he arrived at the spot where their horses were tied, before absconding with Tombo and Annie.

Most probably, the Indians would put one child in front of them on each horse, and return from where they started, or where there may be a camp or village.

He finally found the tracks and the horsedroppings, indicating in which direction they had departed. Bart was determined to catch up to these nefarious beings before they reached any destination. He knew Indians prized captured children and felt they would not harm them.

CHAPTER 15

The rains in Hartley county slowly turned to snow, and then the cold weather moved on east, and the snow started its melt down, nurturing the earth and coloring the stems of the prairie grasses.

Kate finished her fifth hand-rolled cigarette since she'd awakened this morning, while she spooned out some chicken scraps into the saucer to feed Elizabeth.

Elstun finished the milking and placed the pail of warm milk in the spring house, set it next to the separator, and put a square of cheesecloth over it, and returned to the barn.

He emptied the rest of the sack of dry meal and added some scraps of jerky into a tub in the barn, and called in the dogs.

When he finished this chore, he forked some of the stacked timothy hay to the sorrel draft team, and broke the ice-skim on both the water barrels. He went to the chicken pen and checked out all thirteen hens, an picked up nine eggs.

On his way to the back door, Elstun passed a line of clothes hanging outside, frozen stiff to their wooden pins, on the line where Kate left them yesterday. He thought about taking them inside, but he had three of the eggs in his side pocket and the other six in both hands.

"Kate," he called.

"I'm in chere," she answered.

"Well, kin you abide a-gittin' these here aiggs from me, whilst I take down the warshin', which is froze solid."

"If'n yore froze solid, then ,whyn'cha step inside?

"Kate!"

"What is it, Els? I'm a-feedin' Elizabeth her mornin' vittles."

"Kate, hit's a little airish out chere, and I cain't open the door knob 'thout a-droppin' these here aiggs, an' I ain't froze solid, hit's the warsh, that you forgot, is."

"Okay, hit's okay to come in now."

Elstun laid all six of the eggs on the bench beside the back door, and then proceeded back to the clothes line to attempt to take off the laundry that was stuck, and bring it all inside.

He had two pillow cases, three bath towels and two hand towels loosened, and stacked them flat, on top of one another. Next, he reached for the two pair of 'long-johns' and the blue and white night gown hanging along side, and piled them on top of his stack. The underwear legs were sticking straight out when a gust of wind blew the towels away.

As he reached for the towels, the pillow cases wrapped into his face, and his two dogs came out from the barn at the same time.

Pained, Elstun hollered, and the dogs commenced to howl and growl at a sight that was befuddling to them.

Dusty, the blue-tick, lunged for Elstun and suddenly, both dogs jumped at him, causing him to fall. It was lucky none of the three remaining eggs were broken.

"Is 'at you, Els?" Kate hollered.

"Whoo-ee," Elstun sighed, once he was inside lounging in his favorite old rocking chair in their sitting room. "Jest past daylight, and ahm tard, a-reddy."

As always, there was an inordinate amount of work that must be accomplished, to keep a spread such as theirs, or any ranch or farm in abeyance, for as long as this homestead had been engaged.

It became increasingly difficult for Elstun and Kate to communicate with any semblance of sanity, with both facing the anxiety-filled days waiting for Barton Dan'l to arrive home.

"Ahm gonna have yer breakfas' fixed in 'bout a minit'r two, Els, ya heah?"

"Good. I bl'eeve I'll have that braid you made as toast-es, hon. Putt it in the stove fer a tad, an' ahl eat it with some 'Ol' Ned' and aiggs."

"I am a-fixin' that fat pork, but I only picked up six aiggs from the bench."

About that time, Elstun remembered the three eggs in his pocket, and carefully removed them, remarkably still unbroken.

"Ya know, Kate, that rain we'uns had last week was sure a fence-lifter. Ahm sort'a glad the weather chilled down fer the snow. It 'us makin' the fields purty murky. But hit did fill them tanks o'ours."

"Hit warn't near as bad a thet goose-drowner we had two year ago. That was rat turrible. And 'nother thang, the snow's set off, an' I bl'eeve we ain't gonna git no more rain'r snow," rat now."

"Near as I figger," Elstun spoke, "that stage was due in Amariller yesterday or mebby today. If'n hit was late, they'd probably lay-over in town, but if'n hit was early, Bart'd want to high-tail it fer the ranch. So, Kate, I reckon they may just show-up any time from now."

"Ah shore miss him," Kate remarked, "I'll bet he'll stay here this time."

"Well, I knowed he had him a good job with them textile people down south in Presidio. Reckon hit depends on what he decided to do 'bout that. Wonder what she's like?"

"Who?"

"The Meskin gal he married-up with."

"Kate, Ah thank I'll slip on off to the river whilst hit's still early, an' take mah shotgun. Ah seen a mess o' wild Canada geese headin' south, yesterday evenin', an' I'm shore they'll be a few flocks stoppin' to feed on that millet by the banks, there."

"You takin' them dawgs with ya?"

"Kate, them dawgs is hounds, they ain't bird dawgs, or retrievers."

"You best take 'em anyways. They'll run off on their own, onest you leave."

"You're right, hon. I may run acrost a antelope or a bear. Hit ain't time fer them to den-up yet. Anyways, we need to stock up on our meat locker, with them young folks due purty soon."

Elstun took a sack of shells, and his wool-lined, canvas-covered outer coat, and stomped on his double-patched, briar-cut, hip-high wading boots, held up with tan braces.

Els also wore a cartridge belt and a holster with his .44-.40 caliber pistol. He whistled for the dogs, raised his hand shoulder high, in a wave to Kate, and said, "Ah'll see you at chore time afore supper, hon." It was a half mile to the river.

Blam! Blam! His shotgun spoke twice as he reached the first bend of the Rita Blanca river. He was only about fifty yards from the edge when he saw the brace of geese flying in, wings spread, legs dangling down, ready for a water landing. One dropped, one flew on.

"Thar flies a dead goose," Elstun spoke aloud, as he laughed to himself. Instantly, Biff and Dusty raced each other to be the first to arrive at the water's edge, where the honker fell dead.

Elstun was running as fast as he possibly could, in his double-patched, briar-cut, hip-high, wading boots. Both dogs reached the bird simultaneously, and began tearing apart the prey. Feathers were flying and the dogs were growling, and the Canada goose was being torn apart. Elstun was sweating from the energy expended, and swearing at both his hounds, reprehending their act.

"Damn dawgs, meat's hard 'nuf to come by, 'thout you messin' me up. Looky thar, whut you done." Elstun tied-up the dogs, and set down to wait for more geese to fly over his way.

CHAPTER 16

Bart's grulla-dun horse moved as smoothly and as sure-footed as a cougar over the sand plates covering the northwest side of these higher plateaus. He figured the Indians were not expecting anyone to to pursue them, and felt he was gaining on them, noticing the freshness of the horse droppings on the trail.

At this point, Bart was higher than the captors, due to the slight downward trend of the trail. He had to spot them first, for he knew if he was seen, it would surely mean disaster for the children. However, if these were Kiowa, they could decide to take them along to their home territory, farther north.

Bart spotted them. Two Indians, both mounted with the captive children, one on each horse. He felt they were less than half a mile in front.

"Whoa, Blue," he quietly spoke to his horse, as he quickly dismounted. Bart had been trailing these Indians for almost two hours, and about two miles back, they turned west-north-west. He thought they were heading for the Tierra Blanca river, and on to the Kiowa grasslands on the North Canadian river in New Mexico. The closest Army fort was at Raton.

Suddenly, he noticed the Indians had stopped and were resting. Now was his big opportunity to move closer. Bart trailed down the back side of a small hill and he approached them from down wind.

In the next fifty yards, Bart dismounted, and crept slowly to their camp. The Indians had tied both the children's hands and secured them to the base of a small sapling near some brush.

Ten yards away, the Indians were sound asleep, as their hobbled horses grazed, nearby.

One of the Indian ponies nickered when Bart crept forward, but he stopped when Bart laid flat, and remained perfectly still for a moment.

Tombo saw him first, and then, Annie saw him, and she started to grin and say something, but Bart placed his finger to his lips and motioned for her to be quiet.

Ever so quietly, Bart raised himself to a crouched position, and crept closer to the sleeping red devils. As simple as could be, Bart's .44-.40 pistol barked two times, at a very close range. The body of the first one shot, jerked up and back, and left the brave with no face. The next shot entered the second man at his ribs and veered out his side.

The Kiowa sprang to his feet and he reached inside his leggings for the long knife that was tied to his moccasin top. Bart fired again, and the cartridge didn't expend. he threw his gun aside, and he too, reached for his own knife.

The Indian threw himself at Bart and managed to knock him off his feet. The children watched in astonishment, and Annie could only cry. They were also in some pain because the bindings on their wrists were tied to tightly.

"Watch out," cried Tombo, as the Indian threw up dirt with one hand, while his other still held his knife.

"U-ekåa tå, Ya- yekå tå," shouted the red man, while he plunged his knife into the deltoid muscle on Bart's left shoulder. He'd raised his arm to ward off the blow, and the knife slid along the anterior of his upper arm, and tore the flesh with a rip.

The Indian was straddling Bart's body, and was attempting to cut a portion of his scalp, while grabbing a handful of hair and using a swiping motion with his knife in hand.

Bart's adrenalin was pumping hard. His cut arm not a paramount disability for the reserve strength he possessed. With one quick move, and a very powerful thrust of his right fist, Bart knocked the warrior away with a smashing punch to his face.

The two lay momentarily exhausted; the Indian, trying to shake the whirling feeling his brain was emitting, and Bart, regaining his strength for an additional onslaught. He knew his revolver had misfired, and although it lay beside him, he chose to jump the Indian once more, and with his field knife, slit his throat.

The gristle sounded with a snap as if bones were crushed. A gush of crimson blood spewed forth from a severed gullet, and Bart let go the body, as it fell away into the brush and dirt.

He wiped the blood from the knife on the side of his britches before he severed the hair rope that bound the children to the tree. He quickly cut all the ropes from their wrists and freed them. Annie was still sobbing and Tombo was not sure whether to laugh or cry.

Although the kids were frightened beyond scope, they soon settled down, and were beginning to ask questions. Too many.

They both followed Bart as he made his way to where he'd left his horse. He managed to retrieve a long, rolled, card of cotton from his saddlebag that was used to wrap a severe rock cut his horse incurred at one time.

Annie poured some water from his canteen on his shoulder wound, as he instructed Tombo how to wind the wide roll of bandage around his upper arm, and split the end and back-tie it off. "I want my mother," Annie announced, as she was being lifted to the back of one of the Indian ponies. Bart only told them that they were all going back to where the stage coach was, and that they would both be all right. "Thank God," he sighed aloud, "you kids weren't harmed."

Bart tied Annie to the girth rope on the horse she rode, and sat her on a red, doubled-up saddle blanket. Tombo was very capable of riding bareback, and was also able to hand guide his pony with the rawhide, single thong placed around the pony's jaw.

The Indian ponies were well broken and they behaved fine, despite the odor of a non-Indian on their backs. Bart mounted and led the pony Annie rode.

It was very late in the afternoon, and the children had nothing to eat. The Indians had given them some berries and water when they first started out. Bart gave them both the rest of his water. Now they would have to wait until they reached the coach before they could get any more water or food. It promised to be very rough and long journey back.

The ride to the rocky area where the stage was must have seemed a lifetime to Tombo and his sister, but they were very brave and resolute, albeit young, and tired siblings. Bart was concerned , not only with informing them of their mother's death, but also, the well-being of Rosalita and all the rest.

It was very late, a bit cool, and dark enough that it called for caution to get close to the stage coach. Bart approached the area from the very place he took off when he went in search for the Indian kidnappers. First of all, he heard no shots from the stage area, and he was certain there were no Indians on the back side where he rode in.

He stopped, dismounted and hid the children and the horses in a section of heavy brush and some piñion pines. Bart silently walked to a point where he would be able to see and call to anyone near the coach area. Finally, he spotted the coach and teams, and called to Lynx.

"Bart! That you?" Lynx hollered. "C'mon in. Hey, everybody, C'mere, hurry."

Bart was leading the horses with the children mounted on the Indian ponies, as everyone gathered by the stage coach. Rosa ran as fast as she could to reach Bart, and pulled up short when she saw his torn sleeve and his bandaged shoulder. "Oh, *quérido mio, alma,* I ahm so hoppy to see you. I'm so hoppy to see *los niños.* The children, are they all right, they are *no herir,* not hurt?"

The next thirty minutes was the most difficult time in Bart and Rosa's relatively young lives. The children were extremely tired and hungry, and kept on asking for their mother. When they were captured, they didn't realize that their mother was slain at that time. Rosa explained the tragedy as best she could, holding little Annie in her arms, while Bart and Walker tried to solace Tombo.

They eventually got some food into the children and stayed with them until they both cried themselves to sleep.

CHAPTER 17

Daylight was close to appearing, and the yellowness of dawn emerged from the eastern-most side of the rocky hide-a-way where the stage coach remained standing.

Lynch had long ago unhitched the teams of six horses, and they were hobbled and grazing nearby, with the saddle horses.

"If we're going to be attacked this morning, it's likely they'll come at us out of the east, with the sun directly at their backs; harder for us to see them."

No sooner was this spoken, than the cowboy shouted, "Uh, oh, here they come."

They were riding fast, side by side, but with a space of ten yards between the horses. There were six that Bart could make out, and they were literally screaming at the top of their lungs. Of course, this was mainly done to work themselves into a frenzy and provided them false courage.

Close enough now, for them to shoot their arrows, as they rode ahead.

Carrington was struck in his left shoulder with an arrow, and it caused him to lose his balance from where he was standing, and he fell into the rocks next to himself. He must have hit his head when he fell, and Lynx thought he was dead when he saw the blood flowing.

Lynx managed to reach him and determine he was, in fact, not dead, merely knocked unconscious, and Lynx thought this was the right time to try to extract the arrow from him.

The Indian that shot him was making a second pass in their direction, so Lynx stopped his proceedings and fired his shotgun at the brave.

The blast found it's pellets covering the torso of the Indian, and swept him backward off his pony. He was dead when he fell to the ground, and his horse was hit many times with the shot the gun pattern threw. The pony was dieing and neighing pitifully.

One of the red devils was riding toward the area where the coach horses and the saddle horses were hobbled, but Walker spied him and fired a deadly shot into his painted body.

Rosalita shouted to Bart to look back to his left, where another mounted hostile was scampering his pony down the side of the hill where the travelers were all grouped.

The reloaded .44-.40 pistol Bart had used earlier, spoke twice at the oncoming Indian, striking him full in his chest with both shots.

Bart quickly ran to his quarry, to make certain the renegade was dead. He would not have to waste another cartridge on this one. Bart figured this Indian must be the leader of this band. Not only did he ride the largest and best of all their horses, he was dressed much more pretentiously.

The soft, well-tanned leggings and the high-top moccasins were made of elk, not deer. His upper body was stripped to the waist, save for double, porcupine quill, ornamental chest cover. His wrists were wrapped with buffalo-hump leather, and his face was painted so that the lower half was black and red. He wore four, upright eagle feathers in his hair.

Bart straightened up from his examination of the fallen man to find Rosa by his side. She was very careful of his superficial wound as she reached her arms upward and around his neck.

"Oh, Bart-Bart." she sighed, "*Yo no mucho asustar.* I am not scared so much no more. Chu are my he-ro." She kissed him again, with as much passion as possible under the happenings.

Bart responded with equal kisses for his beautiful, dark-eyed sweetheart he'd married. A thought crossed his mind as to whether he had placed her in too precarious a position, together with this involvement of travel to reach his home ranch in Hartley county.

"Oh, *alma mia*, sweetheart, everything will work out all right. We'll have to get the children to their grandparents and that may delay us even some more, but first, we have to win our battle right here."

The three remaining Indians, feeling the fire-power of the group splinter their force, and obviously, slay their cohorts, instantly fled for their lives. They didn't even attempt to recover their dead brothers.

The three rode from the rock-laden escarpment the same way they entered, whipping their ponies and yelling to each other. They had to take the final trail past the outcropping of rocks where Walker Barnes was stationed.

He was watching them approach and he carefully drew a bead with his rifle on the Indian in the rear, and closest to his position. The pony the brave was riding was a Tobiano pinto. A stout animal with a sure-footed stride through the rocky terrain, and Barnes, raised his eye sight on the rifle, so as not to hit that horse.

Walker was hidden from the fleeing red men, and he waited until the last second before he stood beside a boulder and carefully aimed.

A direct hit to the chest dropped the savage to the prairie floor, and when the other two heard the shot, they didn't even slow down, but sped faster to make their getaway. They were riding as if a centaur, one with their horses; stretched flat along the animal's back and neck.

The Indian pony stopped when his rider fell, as he was obviously trained to do. The long rein that was attached to the leather thong around his lower jaw, dropped or was pulled to the earth when his rider was thrown from the force of the rifle shot. A cue for him to stop.

Walker instantly slid down the side of the small embankment and called softly and steadily to the horse. His intention was to capture the animal and take him along with the other Indian pony already in his possession.

It became apparent that the rein of terror attempted by the Indians was truly thwarted, and by everyone's count, the two hostiles that fled would pose no more of a threat to their existence.

It was still early morning when the children awoke and were comforted by the assurance that the Indians were gone and would not return. Rosalita had been busy with dressing Carrington's wound, and turned her attention to the children.

Lynx had a coffee fire going, and he went to the coach and brought a box with some dried fruit and beef jerky to distribute for everyone.

With some food under their belts, and a sense of relief from the attack, they all agreed it was past time to make ready their journey on to Hereford and then to Amarillo. They held services for Ruby at the grave dug by Bart and Walker. Bart spoke of the future, not only for the children, but for all present, and gave thanks for the time spent as a family.

Lynx approached the group and said he was certain the Indians were Kiowas.

CHAPTER 18

By ten o'clock the morning was slowly turning a gray color, and fresh snow was falling on the stage, now back on the road toward the Hereford way station.

The wind set forth it's might and sent th snow blowing from north-east to south-west, slowing the well-rested coach horses somewhat more than Lynx wished.

Walker was no longer sitting atop the stage with the driver, he and Bart were riding the grulla and the bay mare, and herding the captured Indian ponies to keep up with the stage.

Inside the coach, Martin Carrington was trying to comfort himself and appease any pain from his shoulder wound, while abiding the semi-rough ride of one of his own company's stage.

Rosalita was doing her best to offer him comfort and at the same time, tending to the needs of Annie and Tombo. They were still very upset and confused by their mother's death.

Walker was using the mare that Bart bought for Rosa to the best of it's capabilities. She was a young mare that was four years old, but perfectly easy to handle; gentle and well broken.

Bart suggested that Walker put the rope halters he'd fashioned on the Indian ponies, and place one of the ropes in and through each of the halters, this made it easier to control all four of the horses. One was Comanche, and three were Kiowa bred.

Rosalita appeared at the window on the right side of the coach, and caught the attention of Bart when he rode closer to the coach. She smiled, and she motioned him to ride closer.

"What do you need, sweetheart?" he asked, while leaning from his saddle.

"I theenk Señor Carrington needs more attention than I can offer," she replied. "His wound has opened and he's been bleeding, too. He hasn't say much, bot I theenk he maybe is not so very good."

"We just can't afford to stop any more, even for him," Bart replied, he'll have to endure it 'til we reach Hereford."

Bart stood in his stirrups, as he rose up to shout to Lynx, who was driving the now sweating teams of horses.

"No way," answered Lynx. to Bart's query as to whether they should stop just to check on Martin Carrington.

"It ain't but 'bout four to five more miles to the Hereford station," said Lynx, "an' he can shore wait 'til we git there."

As the coach rapidly neared the station, young Tombo had climbed from his seat inside. He crawled through on the opposite side, when Rosa was busy talking to Bart, and placed himself on the drivers bench next to Lynx.

"Kinda dangerous, kid," Lynx said to the boy, who by now was all smiles. "You just be careful, and hold on tight, then you'll be fine."

Walker observed young Tombo and waved back at him with his dusty cowboy hat, and Bart saw him, too. He just smiled and shook his head in disbelief that the lad crawled up on top of the moving stage. He was happy for Tombo, and figured Carrington was hurtin' too much to fuss.

It was very late in the afternoon when the stage pulled into the station at Hereford, in Deaf Smith county, on the panhandle plains of Texas. There was one more day left to travel on to Amarillo. This country was over three thousand and six hundred feet in elevation, and when the winds blew in they brought some mighty cold weather in the winter, to contrast with the summertime hot months.

The travelers experienced the strong winds most of the afternoon, as they came closer to the station. The crispness of the early winter settling in, caused the men outside the coach to cover most of their faces, to stave off the grit and the fierce cold the wind brought along.

Lynx pulled reins and tied the lines to the brake handle before he climbed down to meet the hostler at the way station.

Bart and Walker were busy corralling the saddle horses, and Rosalita had her hands full to prepare Annie and Tombo for their nights stay.

Will and Ella Carter were the station managers, and they took Carrington inside to tend to his condition.

This stage stop at Hereford, Texas, was one of the newer ones built by the Buffalo Lake N & W Railroad, who leased track from the Southern Rail Company. The lease covered rail lines from Childress, Texas, to Tucumcari, New Mexico, Territory.

The railroad began in Shreveport, in Louisiana, and proposed to run one hundred and sixty-five miles beyond Tucumcari, to Albuquerque. Shreveport was a major supply source center for the Confederacy during the four years of the difficult war between the states.

Buffalo Lake was a small lake about half-way between Hereford and Amarillo, and some eastern philanthropists banded together to build this railroad to eventually connect the deep south with the California coastline. They felt the

Hereford station would be one of several on the way from Lubbock to Amarillo, and also from Portales to Amarillo.

The laying of railroad tracks was another reason the Indians were having a hard time adjusting to any reservation life. Many of the track lines were being laid through traditional Indian hunting and burial grounds.

Rosalita was softly sobbing when she finished telling Ella Carter of the awful situation the children had experienced, when Bart appeared at her side.

"Chu are my strength, my hosban'. Chu are brave and re-sourse-a-ful, and I am truly always forever *agradecida*." Rosa was trying to compose herself, while she wrapped her arms around her stalwart husband.

Bart spoke to the station manager's wife, while he was comforting Rosa, and he did so while speaking across the top of her head, holding her gently but firm.

"We'll be out of here as soon as we can in the morning, ma'am," he stated. "It seems as if we've experienced a few bad times on our way to Amarillo. My wife told you about the children's loss of their mother, and that's been a source of real tragedy for us all. I reckon our one thought is to somehow get those kids to their grand-folks, safe and sound."

"Where's their father?" Ella Carter asked.

"Good question," Bart replied.

CHAPTER 19

Will Carter knocked on the door to the room that housed Rosalita and Bart.

"I'm sorry to bother you," Carter said, "but the sheriff and his deputy are here and want to talk to you about that passenger, Carrington."

Bart opened his door a crack, and so as to not awaken Rosa, softly whispered.

"Why don't you get Carrington to answer the questions?" He replied.

"Well, sir, he's not in his room and the bed hasn't been slept on."

It only took Bart a moment to stomp on his boots and step into his britches, then he grabbed his hat and woolen shirt, strapped on his gun belt and joined Will Carter in the parlor.

Lynx and Walker Barnes were already standing in the hallway, talking with the sheriff, who was standing in the parlor doorway. When Bart finally did appear, the sheriff turned around, and Bart saw it was Sheriff Towne, from Clovis.

"This is a surprise, Sheriff," Bart said, as he stood against the wall next to Walker.

"Well, we figured you were already in Amarillo, but the stage people said you hadn't arrived, so we started to back track to Buffalo Lake, then here, to the Hereford station. Mister Walters and the cowboy, filled us in on the mess you all encountered since we departed over at the Sunnyside station."

"What's going on now?" Bart wanted to know. Sheriff Towne then explained how the Army deserter was caught and told how Buffalo McCormack was planning to use his cousin, Amos Sutton, to help him. Buffalo knew Sutton had access to the company's money, so he suspected that Sutton and the owner were in on the whole deal . . . together."

"What deal?" Bart asked the sheriff.

"We figured Carrington had money to pay a crooked Indian agent to give him a big percentage to the Indians to buy guns, so the Indians would keep the railroad from encroaching on their hunting grounds."

"Yep!" Walker replied. "The Indians will chase off the railroad, and ol' Carrington will be able to keep his stagecoach routes from losin' money to any of them ol' railroad boys."

"That's it!" Lynx chimed in. "The boss was stealing money from his own company to furnish the Indians with enough to buy the guns that McCormack and the Army deserter stole."

With this, Walker spoke up and said, "Now, we probably know whut ol' Mistuh Carrington was a-caryin' in that thar black satchel he kept on a-huggin'."

The sheriff and his deputy were sure they were on the right trail, but their desire to question Martin Carrington was thwarted by the disappearance of the suspect, and any evidence must be found to support the motive theory.

The six men buttoned their outer coats and went outside to the stables. As they well figured, one of the piebald Indian ponies was missing, along with a saddle and two blankets.

"Wouldn't ya know," Walker replied, "Ol' Carrington took the best ol' pony."

"What time did you folks finish with supper tonight?" Sheriff Towne asked.

"Well, I 'spect it wuz near 'bout eight o'clock," Will Carter responded. "I know the coach didn't arrive 'til 'bout half-past six, this evenin', and we had the stock to put up and baggage to unload and everyone put to their rooms, and Ella had only h . . . "

"Was Carrington with you at supper?" the sheriff wanted to know, as he interrupted the hostler. "I understand he was suffering a wound he'd received in an earlier conflict you were in."

"Yes, he was," Bart said. "My wife re-dressed the wound in his shoulder, and although he'd lost quite a bit of blood, he said he was feeling much better, and was extremely anxious to reach Amarillo tomorrow."

"Well, it's about eleven-thirty now -so, depending on when everyone retired, he could have left anytime after, oh, say nine o'clock. That'd put him, at least, two hours or more in a head start in whichever direction he's headed."

Bart said he'd bet it would be Amarillo.

"Boys,' the sheriff related, "My guess is the same as Mister Calhoon's. I figure our suspect is headin' to Amarillo and if he's hurting as bad as I think from his bleeding wound, he'll likely stop in Buffalo Lake. Old Doc' Stebbins is the settlement doctor there, and he keeps his office right where he lives."

"You a-fixin' to head out after him rat now, Sheriff?" asked Walker.

"Yep, my deputy and I have sworn to uphold the law, and this duty comes under the provision we both agreed on. He's not much more than two or three hours ahead of us, and if he stops at Doc Stebbins, we can expect to have our prisoner before morning's first light."

"We'll stop at the doc's place in Buffalo Lake," said Lynx. "Might be a good place for us to water and rest the livestock, too."

"We won't wait for you at the lake. If we find him, dead or alive, we'll take him on to the jail in Amarillo. We're gonna need some papers signed and some questions answered, so look me up when you get settled," the sheriff said.

Within ten minutes from the sheriff and his deputy's departure, the four men decided to turn in, and agreed to leave early the next day.

Rosalita helped Ella Carter get the children settled after their meal, and bedded them in the single bed across from the innkeepers room. There, the two women discussed the the events for a while, before they both retired.

Evidently, Rosa didn't awaken when Will Carter woke Bart, for she was sleeping soundly when Bart returned to their bed an hour later.

Bart awoke just before first light, and looked into the soft, and alluring brown eyes of his beautiful wife. They both smiled, and with unspoken words, enfolded arms to one nother, careful to retain the quietness of the morning.

"Oh, my hosban', I am so very lucky to have chu, and I wish for us to make love together right away." Bart thought she was so beautiful at early dawn, as he thought she always was, no matter where or when he was with her. He told her so just before he ardently kissed her.

The wind was fiercely forcing its wrath over this part of the west Texas, panhandle plains, making the start of the journey for the stage extremely difficult.

Jimson weed and some sage was mixed with the sandy grit that stung the cheeks of all who faced the blowing gale. Most of the vision was greatly impaired, not only for the people, but also, for the livestock.

Walker was doing his best to keep the string of, now three, Indian ponies together, and Bart was helping him.

Lynx had the six-up pulling steadily, but the wind, especially as relentless as this, always causes concern for the horses. Their hearing is sensitive, and sometimes the wind causes them to think they hear noises they can't always identify. This often leads to them 'spooking' at things they would ordinarily pass by.

Each of the harness sets Lynx used on the coach horses were equipped with head-stall, eye-blinders, limiting their vision to a more front-ahead field; however, the wind was definitely causing some havoc, and could prove to be very hazardous.

CHAPTER 20

Kate stubbed another hand-rolled, tobacco-stuffed cigarette in her white, porcelain ash tray, before she went to the kitchen to put out some food for Elizabeth's supper. The wind was as loud as a circus caliopé, and caused her to shake and shiver, as it forced its way inside through the cracks and crevices, under the doors and around the windows.

"You both'n ort to git back chere by the far-place, Kate. Hit's rat coolish out thar in yore kitchen."

"I'm a feedin' Elizabeth her supper, Elstun, she don't take it in thar by the far-place, she takes it rat'chere whar she always does. You don't eat in thar, you eat in the kitchen. Now, thet's whut you allus said to me."

"I ain't no kitty-cat, Kate. I'm a growed-up person, whut sits at a table to take mah food. That cat kin eat in the barn, fer alls I kere. Both them dawgs do."

Elstun left the supper table and made his way back to his cedar rocker, while Kate lit another of her cigarettes, before she brought the dirty dishes from the table to the basin beside the kitchen sink.

The water she'd boiled on the stove top was whistling with steam from the old kettle, and she turned and poured this on the plates and flatware that was in the basin.

Kate was almost out of lye soap and decided she'd better make some more, especially since they'd soon have company.

"Whut's thet, you're a-doin', hon?" Kate asked her husband, as she dried her hands on her apron front while she walked into the sitting room where Elstun was rocking.

"Ahm a-readin', Kate." Els laid the spread-open book, face down, when he answered his wife. "This here one is about a pathfinder and his troubles back yonder in the Ohio and Kaintucky valley. It was writ by a feller named Cooper. He knowed all about them Injuns in thet part of our country. Hit's a book that Bart sent us. Kate, them Injuns ain't as fierce as these here Comanch'. Still, hit's mighty good readin'.

Dusty, suddenly awake, jumped to his feet from a spread-on-the-floor position, and Biff, the Red-Bone, knocked him down as he rushed for the living room and the unbolted, front door. Whatever they heard, they both heard it at the same time. Their husky, hound-dog yodels were loudly emitting from their throats.

"Hesh-up, you dawgs," Elstun spoke as he nearly stumbled over them while following them to the door.

"Whut is it, Els? The evils?" Kate was right behind her husband, and had a tight grasp on his belt, on the back of his trousers.

"Don't rat-ly know. Fetch me the big lantern Kate, I'm a-grabbin' mah gun."

Elstun neck-chained the two dogs together, before he opened the door, while Kate remained behind him with the lantern held high over her head with one hand with her other on his belt.

"Who's out thar, who is it?" Elstun yelled the command over the barking noise the two dogs were making. He saw the horse before he saw the Indian, who was dismounted, and walking with his hand up and palm out, toward the front porch.

"Dag-gum you! That you, Whisperin' Charlie? You're alla time slippin' up on us. Tie up yore ol' pony and come in and sit a spell. Kate'll be fixin' you some bait."

"You shore thet's Ol' Charlie?" Kate said, as she released her grip from Elstun.

"Yep, Kate, it is. I've asked him inside, now, will you fix him some grub?"

"No come in big wick-i-up. You come out, see Charlie, now. Big trouble."

"Wal, I reckon I kin spend you a minute. Whut's all the trouble?"

"Walk close. Listen care-ful. Spirits must no hear Charlie tell white-eyes bad talk," he spoke.

"Ah cain't make out to whut he's a-talkin' 'bout, Elstun, whut'd he say?"

"Kate, you ain't s'posed to hear him. At's the reason they call him Whisperin' Charlie. 'Sides, he's a talkin' at me. Be quite, now, and go on back inside, afore he takes it unkindly . . . I'll tell you whut he's said after he's gone on."

"All right, Charlie, m'boy, whut's this heah trouble all 'bout?" Els asked.

"*Ya-nå* marry Kwhadie sub-chief of Black-Water clan. *Ya-nå* say, Comanch' and Kiowa make heap big medicine together, at Rabbit Ear mountain. *Ya-nå* say hus-band favor other wife, not her. She come back our wick-i-up, quit husband, come stay with mo-ther, squaw of Charlie. She say hus-band kill her if she tell what said at big council fire."

"Well, whut went on at the pow-wow?" Els wanted to know.

"Comanche-Kiowa have many ri-fle and much bullet, to fight tosi-tivo off land. Comanche-Kiowa will have this ma-ny men, times this ma-ny, five times more," the Indian said, as he held up fingers on both hands, indicating five hundred warriors.

"Ya-nå say many braves talk of war on tosi-tivo. They leave Rabbit Ear two dawn from tomorrow to kill all whites on trail from Sen-eca to Ca-nad-ian river, near Am-ar-ill-o. If braves cross river, they go all way south to Here-ford. Ya-nå and her mo-ther, squaw of Charlie, leave at first light for fort at Ra-ton."

"Tell your daughter, thanks fer the warning, but Kate and me'll stick it out at our ranch. I'll ride over to Clyde Rawlings' place in the mornin', and see if'n them and the Farrels, and the Ryans want t'come and fort-up for a few days."

"I don't 'spect them Injuns'll wanna mess with them cavalry sojers from Fort Sumner, neither . . . want some 'baccar, Charlie?"

The Indian grinned and held out his hand, and smiled even more when he said,"Give-um Charlie whusky, too. Long ride."

Elstun motioned Charlie to stay as he went inside to retrieve a sack of tobacco and a pint bottle of bourbon whiskey.

The old Indian was as stoic as an opera critic when he took his well-earned loot and departed without another word.

"All right, Elstun, you tell me what Whisperin' Charlie told you, that made you give him a sack of my tobacca', and that bottle of whisky"

"Ahm a-ridin' over to Clyde's place in the mornin', see if'n them and the Ryans and Farrells' want to come fort-up with us fer a few days. Seems as how the Comanch' is on the war-path, again."

"Oh, no, Els, that Injun scarifies me ever time he comes over t'our place," cried Kate, as she bolted the front door for the first time in months. "I jes never knowed whut made you take up with the likes o'him, anyways."

"Whisperin' Charlie is a good'n to know, Kate. He's been a reservation Injun since the treaty was signed, and he's been friendly to me ever since I pulled him and his skinny ol' horse outta thet bog over yonder by the reservation.

He says his daughter told him 'bout them Kiowas and Comanches fixin' to go on the war-path, and I take it special he rid out chere to warn us'n. Now, don't fret any more tonight, I'll git some hep t'morra."

"I'm skeered, Elstun," Kate repeated. Ah hope there ain't no trouble comes just as Bart Dan'l and his new bride is fixin' to arrive, although, I shore would be proud to have thet son of our'n here. I know he'll pertec' us fer sure."

"When Clyde and Will Farrell and Pat Ryan gits here, and Barton Dan'l arrives, we'll have a goodly amount of firepower."

CHAPTER 21

Martin Carrington was on the dusty trail to Amarillo, and was aware that there was a doctor in the settlement of Buffalo Lake. In fact, he remembered that Jethro Stebbins used to work for his stage line while he was studying to become a doctor, and he wound up marrying a Mormon widow that owned a ranch near Buffalo Lake.

Apparently, his shoulder wound was a lot more serious than he thought. It had become infected, inflamed, and now bleeding a lot more.

Carrington was not adept at riding a horse. He cared very little for them and knew nothing as to how to handle them. He was desperate to make his way to Amarillo as soon as possible, and ignored the wound he'd suffered, when he decided to take the Indian horse.

He was feeling weaker by the moment as he slowly approached the front gate to the Stebbins ranch, and feebly dismounted from the piebald pony. He grasped his black satchel as firmly as he could with one hand, and tried to tie off the horse to the gate post with the other.

When he pulled the rein to tighten it to the post, the horse reacted to his force with great resistance; bolted and reared, striking Carrington a swift blow to his head and wounded shoulder.

The pain was so great he collapsed at once, and was unconscious when Molly Stebbins found him lying beside the gate. She was tending to some morning chores and she noticed two riders approaching on the road from Hereford. They were chasing along, what looked to her as a black and white, saddle horse.

Molly called back to the house for her husband. "Come quick," she cried, as she tried to revive the fallen man lying by her front gate.

"G'morning," the riders called over to Molly, as they dismounted. "I'm Sheriff Towne, from Clovis, out New Mexico way. You must be the doctor's missus. This here's my deputy, Jim Shay. I imagine that's the feller we've been trailin' from back at the Hereford way-station," the sheriff stated, as he walked over to Carrington.

Doc' Stebbins reached the gate about the same time and the lawmen introduced themselves to him, whereupon, the doctor asked, "Just what's going on here?"

"Oh, Jethro, I saw this man lying here moments ago, when i was up by the house, and about that same time I saw these men coming with this spotted pony."

"He's hurt pretty bad," Doc Stebbins remarked, while he examined Carrington. "If you boy's will help me carry him to the house, we can finish our conversation as to what's going on. Molly can take your horses and put 'em in that first corral."

The wounded man was placed in one of the extra rooms in the Stebbins house. His wounds were re-administered to, and he drifted in and out of consciousness.

"He's a little too weak to question just now," the doctor said. "Let's all have some breakfast first."

The sheriff and his deputy eagerly agreed.

The Stebbins were given an explanation by the sheriff for the reasons why he was arresting Carrington, and why he felt he and his deputy should leave and take their suspect along.

They indicated they would place him in jail in Amarillo, and let the federal marshal decide his disposition. It was a long tale, and the stage coach passengers stopping over in Buffalo Lake later today would surely corroborate the story. Sheriff Towne instructed Deputy Shay to saddle the horses and make ready for the journey to Amarillo, but Doc Stebbins insisted the patient was in absolutely no condition to travel, and furthermore, (he must remain until he would release him).

"You know, Sheriff," Doc Stevens mused,

"It seems as though I should know that man. I'm certain I've seen him a long while ago, but I can't place him . . ."

"I figure I'll ride into town and wire the marshal at home," Towne replied. "I may get an answer back before the stage gets in here. In the meanwhile, you just might be thinking on just how you know Carrington."

Lynx had the six-up in a nice, brisk walk, after previously urging them in a faster pace, as he pulled into the depot at Buffalo Lake.

Bart rode with Rosalita and the children in the coach on this leg of the journey from Hereford. Both of the children seemed in good spirits, due in part, to the toys they received from the Carters when they left this morning.

Little Annie coveted her doll that had an extra dress, and she kept busy re-changing this garment all morning. Tombo was given a box of twenty lead soldiers, of which he would position strategically inside the stage coach, pretending a soldier campaign.

Walker Barnes, riding Rosa's bay mare, and herding Bart's horse with the others, spotted the Kiowa piebald in the corral at the Buffalo Lake station, and knew immediately that old Carrington was most likely here. He recognized the sheriff's horse and the one Deputy Shay rode, also penned in the corral.

"Jethro," Molly discreetly said to her husband, as they met in the hallway after everyone else was seated and enjoying a late lunch. "Listen to me. You must remember Lucy and Noah Crawford from Hereford; he's the retired veterinarian that moved to Amarillo last year."

"Well, ah . . .why, yes, I do. What about it?"

That was their son that was shot and killed in that bank hold-up two days ago. The hold-up the circuit rider told us about when he rode through here yesterday,"

"That's right! The Bruner gang! They shot two and the other two got away."

"I was just certain," Molly said, "that their son was in the Army. I don't see how he could've been involved in any bank hold-up, or be with any bad men."

"Maybe I should ask Sheriff Towne what he knows about it," the doctor resolved.

"No, not now. Not while those youngsters are still awake. Remember, their last name's Crawford. Rosa told us about that tragedy with their mother, and their own terrible experience with their capture by the Indians.

The poor dears," she went on, "there's no way we should say anything in front of them. We must find the truth."

After lunch, Lynx Walters was ready to get his passengers to Amarillo. He asked the sheriff what plans he had with Mister Carrington, and if there was some attorney that he should contact when they reached Amarillo.

"I guess I better ride over to the telegraph office," the sheriff answered Lynx. "They will probably have an answer to my wire I sent them this morning. Maybe I'll be able to answer your question as to what to do with your boss."

"He was my boss," Lynx chuckled. "I ain't sure what's gonna happen to him from here on out, nor the company, either."

"Uh, Sheriff," Doc asked, "could I talk with you and Lynx and Bart, outside, for a minute, before you all go?"

The men stood by the back corral and talked, while Sheriff Towne was saddling.

Doc Stebbins told the men what his wife said about the Crawfords, and how they wondered what the outcome may be.

CHAPTER 22

In about thirty minutes the sheriff returned from the telegraph office with some very interesting news. The stage was not yet loaded, and would wait now for the news that Sheriff Towne had to relay.

Molly Stebbins was in the side yard with Annie and Tombo who were playing with new, twin baby goats, while everyone else was in front with the stage coach.

"His name is father," Annie answered Molly, when asked her father's name. "Are the goats hungry? What are their names?"

"No, Annie," Tombo corrected, as only a big brother was wont to do. His name is Jason. I can't remember his next name, cuz we haven't seen him for a long, long time. He's a soldier in the U.S. Army, and we're going to see our grandmother and grandfather; that's where my mother was taking . . ." Tombo began to sob, and ran to Molly for her comfort; he was joined instantly by little Annie.

The discussion with the sheriff and the rest was enlightening and yet serious with what was disclosed.

"I have two wires here," the sheriff said, as he read and paraphrased both.

"It seems as there's an inquiry going on with some insurance company and the Pinkerton Detective assigned to examine the books of the Carrington Stage and Transport Company."

Well," Walker spoke up, "Now were a-gonna find out whut the man was a-totin' in that there ol' black satchel of his."

"Also," Sheriff Towne said, "That Army deserter that was involved with this mess through his brother-in-law, escaped from jail last week. They've sent flyers out as wanted posters we can pick up when we get to Amarillo. They also say this deserter is believed to be one of the men that was shot while holding up the bank.

Bart was reading the telegram from over the sheriff's shoulder, and suddenly turned away with an astonished look.

"What is it, Bart?" Walker asked. "Why are you looking so surprised?"

"His name . . . is Jason Crawford."

Molly Stebbins clutched the children unto herself, comforted them and dried their tears. She pointed to the red and white goat kids, and called their names.

"Look, Annie, this one is called 'Daisy', and that one is called 'Buttercup'. I'll just bet you don't know why they're named that."

"I know," Tombo defiantly proclaimed. "That looks like a flower with that red marking on it's back. It sort's looks like a daisy there, but I'm not real sure."

"Hooray for you, Tombo," Molly said, as she mildly patronized him. "How about the other one called 'Buttercup'?"

"Tell us," they both answered.

"We named her that because she would always eat all the buttercup flowers that bloom in the section of the yard where they live."

By now, Molly felt both the children's attention was purloined from the thoughts of their mother and father, and she told them to get themselves ready to go see their grandparents in Amarillo, Texas. "How would you kids like a dish of vanilla pudding before you leave?"

Deputy Shay and Sheriff Towne only preceded the departed stagecoach by ten minutes. They said they wanted to reach Amarillo and speak with the Pinkerton Agency detective.

The Insurance companies usually paid a good fee for the arrest and conviction of any perpetrator of a crime where it involved any of their insured. The two New Mexico lawmen felt they would be entitled to these fees soon.

Along the Amarillo stage trail, Lynx saw what he was certain, the deputy riding back to Doc Stebbins place, where he'd just left.

"What's up, Jim?" Lynx hollered to the deputy, as they approached each other, while he pulled the teams to a halt. "Is there any trouble up ahead.?"

Bart stepped from the coach when it stopped, leaving Rosalita inside with the Crawford children, and walked over to the deputy.

"The sheriff got to figurin' someone better keep an eye on ol' Carrington, in case he decided to skip out on the doctor and his wife, before any lawman could get back and accompany him to Amarillo, so he sent me back. Said he'd wire me in a few days. He wants to talk with the marshal first and some detective that . . ."

Walker Barnes was riding the bay mare as fast as he could, straight for the group assembled at the coach, and interrupted the deputy with some frantic words.

"Hey, y'all," he shouted, almost out of breath. "Almost two miles north-west of here is a huge party of Injuns! There must be near 'bout two hundred horses or more. They're followin' the river, but I seen 'em because of all the dust they're a-raisin'."

"Think they seen you?" Lynx questioned.

"Don't reckon they did. I didn't see nobody come after me. I kept all these-here horses in front of me, and skedaddled here quick's ah could . . . whut're you doin' here, Deputy? I thought the sheri . . . "

"Tell ya 'bout it later," said Bart, heading for the stage to tell Rosalita. "Guess I'd better catch my horse, Walker."

"What d'ya figure it means?" Walker asked Lynx. "You reckon them Injuns is on the war-path . . . . agin?"

"It shore don't sound like no huntin' party. I think we better turn back for the Stebbins place, 'specially with these kids inside here; it'll take us less than an hour to git back there."

"You're absolutely right," Bart agreed. He called inside the stage for his wife, and told her of the circumstances in Spanish, hoping to keep the information from the children, at least until they were safely back at Buffalo Lake.

"*Indîo Comanché* means Indians," exhorted Tombo, as he listened to parts of the conversation Bart was having with Rosalita. "And *pelar grandé,* means big fight. I learned that from my friend, *Pâncho,* back home."

Bart smiled as he shook his head, "I guess there's no foolin' you, big guy. We plan to go on back to the Stebbins ranch, at least 'til we contact the Army and see just what is going on.

"You should try to reach my father," Tombo said. "He could probably save us all."

* * *

Caleb Temple was at the Stebbins' ranch on the outskirts of Buffalo Lake, when the coach pulled back into the corral area, and unloaded. He brought Uncle Jethro and Aunt Molly the news of the Indian uprising from the north.

Caleb had been chief of scouts for major Eugene Carr's Fifth Cavalrymen and Indian scouts and helped deliver a final blow to the Cheyennes in July of 1869, at Summit Springs, in Colorado. He came home to Texas when granted a hiatus due to an injury that recurred on occasions. His decision to remain was reinforced when he finished talking to Lynx and Bart at the stage coach. Caleb's scout friends informed him of the impending Kiowa-Comanche forces on their war paths.

Walker told Caleb what he witnessed this morning on the route to Amarillo, and the decision to return was applauded by Caleb for prudence the red raiders were to turn to the direction of Buffalo Lake, the Stebbins ranch would be an excellent refuge in which to fight.

CHAPTER 23

Rosalita felt a sense of concern as she watched her husband, so serious in his manner, while he double-checked the ammunition and the firepower availability that prevailed among all. She did admire his tenacity and leadership, and finally overcame her concerns as the day lengthened.

A little before supper, Marvin and Maude Atkins drove their team into the ranch with their two teen-aged sons, Philip and Marty, each mounted on a fine saddle horse. The Atkins ranch was about six or seven miles north and west of Doc Stebbins place, and a much smaller homestead.

Marvin howdied everyone when he stepped down from the rig and sought out Doc Stebbins; he wanted to be sure it was all right to bring his family over. He'd seen a lot of sign that Indians were near by, and felt this was a safe move.

Everyone present on the front porch could plainly see the smoke billowing and the early evening sky alight with the red and yellow reflection of flames. It was certain that the McBride's cabins and corrals were on fire. Their homestead was only two miles beyond here.

They were all positive that the Indians were ravaging the valley, and were most likely on their way to Hereford, and the stock yards. Everyone hoped that the settlement of Buffalo Lake was not as helpful to the Indians because of only a few buildings and no stockyards.

Most small ranches surrounding the town would be useful to the Indians with their supplies of food and livestock, and perhaps with ammunition and weapons.

Never-the-less, Bart and Lynx asked Doc Stebbins if they could direct any retaliation, should the savages swing past the town, and pass this ranch on their way to Hereford. This was agreeable, so they started fortifications.

No sooner than barricades were erected, hoof beats and whistling was heard.

No less than four U.S.Army scouts were approaching the Stebbins ranch, and were readily identifiable by the guide-on banner that one scout displayed.

Bart and Doc stepped from behind the front gate to greet the men and inquire of their disposition.

"There's seven companies of Army troops passing here that were dispatched from Fort Sumner and Fort Raton. We're on our way to Hereford to intercept a very large band of Kiowa and Comanche Indians," one of the scouts reported to answer Bart and Doc's questions.

"You may be closer than you think, trooper," Bart said, as he motioned the riders to dismount. "Just a short while ago we saw a near-by ranch on fire, and about four hours ago one of our men discovered a large force of hostiles maybe fifteen miles north of here."

"We won't dismount, sir" said the scout, we must report back to the Colonel as soon as possible. They will want to bivouac nearby tonight, and strike out for the interception very, very early in the morning, sir."

The four rode off toward the troops.

"Seven companies figure as a force of nearly four hundred men," the doctor said to Bart. "I wonder now if the war department has finally decided to place more troops here, in West Texas to help us get rid of these marauders, and let the railroads commence their progress out here."

"It would likely take over three thousand men, divided into companies of fifty or fifty-five each to sweep these borders from north-west Texas south into the New Mexico territory border," Bart suggested.

"This force is roughly only about ten percent of the figure needed to wipe out the remaining Comanche," he stated.

"If the Colonel the scout referred to is Colonel Roland Archer, he may be able to get the job done with even less troopers." Doc said to Bart. "I read a paper he wrote and sent to his brother in Lubbock, that detailed his plan for troopers on field maneuvers. I'm certain Archer was commanding at Fort Bascom, on the Red river before he was stationed at Fort Reno. He's a real stickler for austere warfare."

Walker joined the two men at the front gate when the Army scouts rode off, listening to the conversations between Bart and Doc; Doc continued, "The Colonel wrote that it should be understood that troops (should be ready for arduous service. Rations of coffee, sugar and everything but hard bread, beef and tobacco, should be stopped while they were in the field, and their pay increased).

"He said, (a trooper's horse should not be cumbered with useless holsters and a lot of extra harness for display, The soldier should carry two Colt's pistols. a first-class Spencer carbine, and a long knife. The Commissary should keep bales of bread and meat of sixty pounds a bale, and enough for ten days rations for men).

"He also stated, (there should be pack mules enough to carry these provisions, with no more than two packs to a mule)."

Walker Barnes was astonished at the detail in which this was presented, and said he thought with these precautions the soldiers could indeed, "pursue and conquer them 'wily, ornery red devils.'"

The four scouts caught up with the Army troopers and reported what had been told them by the folks at the stage coach station at Buffalo Lake. The Colonel then ordered a halt and immediate bivouac, in order to make the preparations for the next day's foray.

The large band of Indians, made up of Kiowa and Comanche, and a few dozen Arapaho and Utes, made their way to the south banks of the Palo Duro Canyon. Game was plentiful through this land surrounding the river and the canyon, where they eventually made camp.

These Indians were comprised of mostly Kwahadie Comanche, some of whom fought in 1870 against a group of Texas Rangers, who under the command of Captain Sul Ross, surprised the band on the desolate banks of the Pease and caused them to fall back north, across the Canadian river. Many Indians agreed, by the 1867 Medicine-Lodge treaty, to come to the reservation, but not the leader of this band whose name was Quanah Parker, the very most ferocious of the tribe.

With the assurance that the U.S. Army was in nearby bivouac, all the people gathered at the Stebbins ranch on the out skirts, rested well.

Rosalita and Molly Stebbins took turns in keeping company with little Annie and Tombo Crawford, and each took turns to rest by the room where the children slept.

Everyone that had not yet arisen the next morning, was suddenly awakened by the sound of yelling and gunfire out in front. First light presented a large band of seventy Indians assaulting the Stebbins ranch.

Walker was one of the first to hear the renegades, and also one of the first to fire any shots at them, He was soon joined by Lynx who was sleeping in the stage parked near the corrals. The two Atkins brothers were bunked at the barn, and were able to take cover there, while shooting at the Indian horde.

Caleb, Marvin Atkins and Bart made their way out to the barricades, while inside, the women looked after the children. Doc Stebbins got his shotgun and sat in the same room with Martin Carrington. The fighting had begun.

CHAPTER 24

The band of Indians involved in the fighting at the Stebbins ranch planned their foray to include sacking the place and also the supply and feed store in town. Obviously, a few of the Arapaho's that joined the group as scouts, had been in this area as 'friendly Indians', at an earlier time; later to spy for the Kwahadies.

The problem the folks defending the ranch had was about twenty-five Indians in the band were equipped with M1849 repeating rifles; however, their ammunition was limited.

The leader of this semi-mixed group of Comanche and Kiowa, was *Tats-ah-Des-o,* trans-lated as the 'Slick Killer'. He was feared by even the boldest of his tribe, and noted for his personal courage. He was very constant in his capricious rule, and he often quarreled with the young Kwahadie chief, Quanah Parker, who was not on this raid, but had sanctioned it at the 'medicine-fire' council held during the night.

Tats-a-Des-o' was easily prominent by the demeanor he presented. He rode in front of the rest; he led by example and he was an excellent equestrian. Most of the Comanche were distinguished by their two-feather head-wear, while the

Kiowa wore a many-feathered bonnet with all the feathers in a circle, standing upright

The neophytes usually did not wear any feathers, but carried twelve foot lances. Each warrior was paint-marked according to his preference.

Onward the screaming horde charged, darting forward and then quickly retreating, often able to discharge their bows and keep as many as eight arrows in the air at one time.

Bart had his two, .44-.40 caliber pistols and his Spencer carbine continually in use. When he fired his rifle, it was to aim at the riders circling toward the back, using his pistols for closer-in targets.

The two Atkins boys were crack shots, and they continued to enact great fire power at the Indians, from their position in the barn loft.

Over at the corrals, eighty yards farther away, and where Walker and Lynx were making a stand, things were not as comfortable. It seems as the two men were in a cross-fire from where the red men ended their charge, and the next wave began. Not so much from the bullets, rather from scores of arrows , some with the ends wrapped and set afire. This ploy was not working at the front and side of the stone house. The Indians simply could not get close enough to effectively send their fire arrows to the main building.

One of the two hay stacks was on fire and the smoke was billowing almost straight up from the lack of any breeze.

Four miles away, on the west banks of the Palo Duro river, where the seven companies of Cavalry were encamped, the smoke was duly noted , and 'boots and saddles' was sounded for D company and H company. The colonel wanted to keep the other five companies in reserve, because his scouts said the main body of hostiles was camped at the head of the canyon.

One hundred troopers plus six of the officers departed the confines of the battalion, with one scout and a bugler. The one hundred and eight cavalrymen of the two companies rode directly toward the smoke they saw eman- ating from Buffalo Lake and the ranch known to them as the Stebbins place.

Fighting at the ranch was continuing with the men behind the barricades doing most of the shooting. This is where the charges started, with a slight arroyo behind an open area of ground covering several acres, and affording the Indians initial cover until the last minute.

Inside, the women were preparing food and water for the fighting men, and insisting the Crawford children remain in the parlor, in the center of the house.

Rosa constantly made her way to the front windows trying to watch for her husband behind the barricades outside. She was bound and determined to pack a pail of water and some food outside during a break in the shooting. Bart was upset with her mulish decision, but he graciously welcomed her appearance.

"Eet ees not so good for us, my hosban'?" she questioned Bart, as she crouched next to him behind the rock and wooden barrier.

"No, not at all, alma mîa," he replied, and reassuring her, urged her to keep her head below the top boards. "We have plenty of ammunition, and I don't think those Indians want to get too close where they become easy targets. Marvin and I have killed three Kiowas, already."

No sooner than Bart spoke, about ten or twelve Comanche appeared at once from the draw, riding straight for the house as fast as their ponies could run.

Four of the mounted bucks rode straight for the barn, several peeled off for the side of the house, and five charged straight ahead to the barrier.

Caleb Temple, was standing and he was sheltered by a spring wagon, tipped on its side with some boards covering it. He was firing his carbine and yelling at the feathered heathens at the same time.

Bart was shooting from the middle and Marvin Atkins was on his right side.

It was a miracle that Rosa was with the men at the barricade. She was invaluable to them. As soon as one would empty a weapon, she would reload for them while they fired their other piece. She watched as Caleb was struck in the arm, and she quickly tied his neckerchief around it to stem the bleeding.

Seconds later, Marvin was hit in the upper part of his leg above the knee with an arrow. Rosalita examined the arrow and found that just part of flint had come through. He asked her to pull it out but she couldn't move it. Since it was painful to Marvin, she asked Bart to help.

Bart took hold of the point of the arrow that was sticking through his leg, and with his other hand hit the feathered end and drove it through. Rosa drenched it with some water, and covered it with part of his torn shirt.

Caleb and Bart both fired at two of the savages, that by now had diverted their charge and were standing with their horses a short way in front of the group, exposing themselves and loudly and profanely touting everyone.

False courage, indeed, thought Bart.

The two Atkins brothers were both excellent shots and the slaughter of the Indians and their horses that approached their sights were many. Two warriors had been shot by Marty Atkins and they were both hit in the head. Their horses lay where they fell, also shot by Marty.

His brother, Phil, figured it was easier to hit the Indians when they were un-horsed, so he repeatedly shot their horses from under them, then carefully drew aim and finished their rider.

Lynx could see the two brothers at the barn, and counted eight or nine dead horses and as many redskins there.

The Indians expected to get the people at the ranch in a very short time and kept charging in their circles. With short intervals they charged on every side at the same time. They thought the ranch folks would fire all their shots and when they stopped to reload, would ride in and massacre them all.

Several of the Comanche left their horses in a ravine to avoid the shooting and crept in toward the ranch corrals. Walker saw them and hollered to Lynx who waved back that he, too, spotted them. The men thought there were only three, but in reality, there were about seven.

Two Comanche warriors rose up from their cover, and rushed the position from where Lynx was shooting. He was busy reloading, and didn't see them until the last moment. It became an immediate hand-to-hand combat at that time.

From high in the barn loft, a rifle shot quickly rang out, and struck the Indian closest to Lynx, directly between his shoulder blades, tippling him to an instant death. Marty Atkins grinned at his brother Philip, who'd sent the shot true.

Lynx was no stranger to hand fighting with Indians. As the next buck leaped forward, Lynx caught him in the throat with his knife for a very effective kill.

The attack on the Stebbins ranch started early, and had been in force for about two hours, when suddenly, almost as quickly as it began, tapered off to where there wasn't even the occasional sniper shots from the Kiowa- Comanche marauders.

Bart contacted each man to make certain there were not any fatal injuries, and he found that Caleb's slight crease in his arm, and Marvin Atkins more serious knee wound, were all that the group suffered.

He made sure Rosalita took Marvin back inside, and told them both to stay there. He called Walker and Lynx to help scatter the remaining hay pile, so it wouldn't catch fire, and checked inside the barn on the safety of their own horses.

Everyone knew now, why the Indians swiftly pulled out, leaving their dead where they fell. Not only could they see the Army troops coming, they could hear the melodious bugle calls, wafting on the late morning breeze. After the troopers arrived, one of the first chores was to haul away the carcasses of the dead horses. Bart reported sixteen dead Indians.

CHAPTER 25

Captain Stuart, who commanded both companies of cavalry, reminded the men at the ranch that while the warriors who had been fighting them fled, the main force of Indians were believed to be still in their camp over in Palo Duro canyon.

He said his troops would remain at the ranch for the remainder of the day, to make certain all was secured, and help with the clean-up details, but they would rejoin their full command before evening time.

Their orders were to to also engage the band of Indians that were in this fight and to return them to the reservation. If they refused, their orders were to destroy them.

The next morning, after an evening's discussion as to the disposition of the Crawford children, it was decided to take them along on the stage coach to Amarillo, and once there, to locate their grandparents. Rosalita wanted to tell Bart what Molly told her about the senior Crawfords.

Doc Stebbins and Bart discussed the situation concerning Carrington, and the doctor said he would be responsible for his patient, and would release him to the federal marshal, after wiring him at a later date.

The more he thought bout it, the more he remembered the injured man named Carrington. He called his wife into the parlor and told her he was certain that the injured man in the bedroom was the same Martin Carrington that he started to work for over twenty-five years ago.

"Do you remember me a-tellin' you that I took a job when I was startin' to go to medical school, when Ida was still alive, before the diphtheria took her. I had a lot of bills to pay, and that was about the time you and Henry bought this ranch. I didn't work for him very long, before I started my practice, but - yep, that was him, all right. That's where I knew him."

"Guess you should tell the marshal that you knew him as a good man, Jethro," Molly said. "He may need someone as a character witness, if he's done wrong."

"They said he stole money," Doc stated.

"Mister Calhoon," Molly Stebbins called to Bart, before everyone was quite ready to leave for their trip to Amarillo. "I think we need to discuss what you and your wife are planning for the Crawford children."

"I guess Rosa and I will take them to Amarillo and try to locate their grand folks," Bart answered to Molly.

"Well, if that's so, I expect you should know that the doctor and I feel certain we know exactly who their grandparents are. It has to be Lucy and Noah Crawford, who moved there from Hereford. Noah was a veterinarian, and decided to retire and move about a year ago.

"He's likely known in town," Bart said." I'll bet another vet or even any blacksmith would know how to reach him."

"I'm sure you'll find them, although I don't know if they're able to care for the children right now. I guess by now that you have figured out that their daddy was the escaped soldier and convict was killed in that bank hold-up. He was Lucy and Noah's son, Jason."

Rosalita realized full well that the responsibility would be with Tombo and his sister, Annie. She and Bart decided they would be totally responsible for the children until they could release them in the care of their paternal grandparents.

*   *   *

The stagecoach departed the Buffalo Lake area and the Stebbins ranch and Lynx drove the well-rested teams, while Walker Barnes again busied himself with the remuda of horses. This time, Walker rode the Tobiano pinto that he originally captured from the Indians, figuring Carrington wasn't about to keep him. He sold one of the other Kiowa ponies to Marvin Atkins before he left, and herded all the other horses along. This included Bart's and Rosalita's horses, Caleb Temple's horse and the other captured Indian pony.

Bart and his wife rode inside with the Crawford children, and Caleb accompanied them, deciding he had some business to attend to in Amarillo. He told his aunt and uncle he'd be back to stay awhile with them in a week or so.

It took Lynx less than four hours to drive the stage into Amarillo. The twenty-seven miles was covered with only one comfort stop, and about thirty minutes to rest the teams. They reined by the huge front porch of the Carleton Hotel, and began unloading all their gear.

Walker choused the horses to the end of the street where the livery was, and as soon as the coach was unloaded, Lynx made arrangements with the company stage office to put up the teams and the coach.

Bart talked with the Pinkerton detective and the insurance investigator about his association with Carrington, and all the other events leading up to Carrington's care at the Stebbins ranch over in Buffalo Lake.

They questioned Lynx Walters, and for that matter, Walker Barnes as well as Caleb Temple. They had already taken a disposition from the New Mexico sheriff.

When the insurance company and the prosecutor determined their findings, the U.S. marshal would be sent to arrest Carrington. Meanwhile, Bart needed to question the sheriff about Jason Crawford.

Rosalita was having some difficulty when she registered with the front desk clerk at the Carleton Hotel. She was not able to write her name or information asked for, or any of the other things in English. The clerk wasn't capable of reading or speaking any Spanish and thought she was trying to get him to give her money from the hotel safe.

Bart entered the front door and upon hearing some of the conversation, reached across the counter, lifted the clerk with an iron grip under both arms, and pulled him to the floor in front of the counter.

Lynx was right behind him and so was the insurance man and the Pinkerton detective. They all grabbed Bart and held him from putting his fist in the face of the horrified clerk.

Rosa sheltered the children at the side of the room, and began to speak in Spanish to Bart, trying to explain the circumstances. After only a moment, the detective, who knew the clerk well, explained it all to his chagrin, and apologies were given and accepted on both sides. Everyone was very tired and a clean room was certainly welcomed.

Lynx was up before the sun and after his morning coffee, headed ver to the Carrington Brothers Stage coach office located on Border street. The Pinkerton detective greeted him, as he rose from his tilted-back, wooden chair at the side of the front entrance.

After a lengthy discussion, Mister Harker, the Pinkerton man, disclosed some vital information concerning Carrington. It seems as though the insurance company and the detective agency had been investigating Martin Carrington for the last five or six months. Pat Packard, the manager of the corporate loan division of the Stockman's Bank and Trust, had discovered some discrepancies in the profit and loss statements. there was short-fall on two account receivable entries, each month.

Carrington, himself, had access to his books and set up phony accounts payable to a false creditor, called Jason and Associates. The company was not yet bankrupt, but an additional infusion of capital was needed to regain their degree of trust with the Stockman's bank.

CHAPTER 26

The Carrington Brothers Stage Coach company was started, in fact, by Martin and his older brother, Merlin Carrington. Six years ago, when Merlin was killed in a coach hold-up that occurred near Kermit, Texas, the business was starting to lose customers to the new railroads whose rail tracks were joining East and West.

Harry Harker, the affable detective, was explaining all this to Lynx, in hopes tat he'd contact Mister Packard at the bank, and somehow, get involved with the new management the bank wanted to set up.

"Just think, Mister Walters," the detective said, "you could become a part owner in this company, and probably be operating manager."

"Well, I'm not sure I'd wa . . ."

"You probably wouldn't have to put any money in the operation, least not yet. The banks' powerful interested in this outfit," Harker interrupted Lynx, "they are sure the company can make 'em some money, provided it's run with a straight hand . . . and you've been with 'em long enough to know all about the operation."

"Well," Lynx mused, "it does sound a little tempting, maybe I'll mosey over to the bank and discuss it. What d'ya 'spose will happen to ol' Carrington?"

"I expect him to be brought to trial and be found guilty of stealin' funds, but more importantly, be found guilty of the sellin' of guns to them Injuns."

"I guess that's the reason the U.S. marshal's in on this," said Lynx. "Well, he's in good hands at Doc Stebbins' ranch . . . 'sides, he's in no kinda shape to run."

On his way to the bank, Lynx passed the restaurant next to the Carleton Hotel and stopped inside when he spied Bart and Rosa seated with the two Crawford children.

He decided to ask Bart his opinion on the decision he'd made to talk to the banker about his involvement with the stage coach company.

"I think it's an excellent decision, Lynx - you're just the right one for the job." Rosalita asked her husband if she could stop in a few of the shops across from the hotel, and take the children along because they need a few things.

Bart thought that was a good idea because he wanted to go with Lynx to see the banker.

"I think the bank man can likely tell us how we might reach the children's grandparents, the Crawfords," he said.

Lynx had another cup of coffee while everyone else finished their breakfast, and then he and Bart headed for the bank.

"Howdy, I'm glad to meet you," the banker spoke to Bart, after being introduced to him by Lynx. "I know your daddy. I loaned him some seed money three years ago, and he paid it all back last year."

"I think," he continued, "you ought to get involved with Mister Walters, here. With the running of this stage company, you see, we could arr . . ."

"No, I'm right sorry to disappoint you or Lynx, Mister Packard," Bart flatly stated. "but I have too many other plans.

Thank you, anyway. It's most important for you to know, however, what a good man you have with Mister Walters."

The banker had some papers drawn up governing the disposition of stock that comprised the majority of shares in the Carrington Stage Coach business, and, pending the final outcome of the trial of Martin Carrington, and the legal affairs all settled, offered these to Lynx for him to strongly consider.

"Now, Mister Calhoon," he turned to Bart and said, "here is a sketch I have drawn to show you how to get out to the Crawford spread. It's probably about five or so miles from town, on the east side."

"Thanks a might," Bart replied. "I reckon I'll check with the livery about gettin' a big wagon to deliver all of us, and get started just as soon as possible."

On his way over to the livery stable, after a positive, good-luck speech and a temporary so-long to Lynx, he caught up with his traveling partner who'd become a very close friend.

"Just the person I wanted to talk with," Bart said, as he beckoned Walker to hold up.

"Rosa and I are fixin' to take the youngsters out to their grandparents ranch east of town, but before we leave, there's a proposition I'd like for you to consider. We plan to be back here this evenin', and leave tomorrow for my folks place up in Hartley county."

'Yep," replied Walker. "I knowed y'all was plannin' to do that, soon's we got to the end of the stage line here in Amiriller."

"Well, what I have in mind concerns you, amigo. I'd like you to accompany us to my folks place, and take root there as a top hand for the ranch. I know my daddy can use some help, and you'd be in a good position to share-crop and run the horse herd, and help alot with the cattle operation."

"Oh, Ah really wasn't a-plannin' on stayin' in this country. I was just a-brokerin' hosses for some outfits in west Texas an a-headin' south, if'n I found a few more."

"Well, Walker," Bart said, as he placed an arm on his shoulder, "I'd really like you to come along and meet my folks, and see their ranch, and listen to an offer, before you make any decision against it."

Walker allowed as how he would.

It wasn't long before the rented wagon and a team was assembled for the late afternoon trip to the Crawford ranch.

Tombo, and his sister, Annie, were so excited to be going to their grandparents ranch, and they looked forward to be able to stay and be taken care of.

Annie had persuaded Rosalita to buy a book of children's poetry she felt sure her grandmother would read to her, and she had it wrapped as a special gift.

Tombo was not to be outdone, and he bought his grandfather a new grass rope, in hopes that he would teach him how to use it.

Rosa took along a large box with some things that belonged to the children's mother, that she'd saved since that one terrible day.

There were two, erect spruce poles holding a cross-bar of a peeled, logan-oak log with a sign hanging from the center, over the main entrance to the Crawford ranch.

'El Rancho Poquîto', the sign read, in hand- carved, rutted-out letters.

Now it was only a short drive to the house.

CHAPTER 27

There was a pall of sadness hovering over the Crawford ranch when the wagon with Bart and Rosa and the two children pulled into the front area of the house and tied the team to a hitching rail.

Lucille Crawford, finally emerged from the porch into the four, outstretched little arms of two bundles of happiness, rushing to grab at the skirts of their grandmother.

"Noah, come quick," she called to her husband, as she at once realized who the four unexpected guests were. Bart and Rosalita politely remained beside their wagon until Noah presented himself.

It only took very few moments for the awful news to be related about the tragedy of Ruby, and who the Calhoons were, and of their quest to bring the children to their original destination.

Unfortunately, the sheriff had paid a visit earlier, telling them about Jason.

After the jubilation from the two children abated, and a good, warm supper was consumed, the adults collected their thoughts and decided to break the news to Tombo and Annie about their father.

Somehow, it didn't seem to register with Annie. Perhaps her age was primarily the reason, and her recall of her father was never on a lasting time basis. Tombo, on the other hand, was adamant that there was some mistake made . . . that his father was a soldier and not involved with the 'bad-men' that caused his death.

Rosalita felt it was almost too much for the children to comprehend, at least for Tombo. First, it was his mother, whom he adored, and then trying to come to terms with the death of his father, of whom he hadn't seen much, but genuinely idolized.

The two women did their best to get the children bedded in, especially Annie. This done, they joined the men to discuss what measures would be taken to have the children remain at the ranch.

As much as Bart was anxious for he and Rosa to get to his home, he was ready to listen to the Crawfords insistence that he and Rosalita stay the night and start tomorrow.

The dawn approached Bart and his lovely, resolute bride of less than a month, with the softness of a pastoral setting, as the sun began to filter its morning rays through the east-facing window.

Rosa's quiet slumber was compromised by the collection of her curvaceous body in the arms of her adoring husband, and held tenderly, while she slowly awakened.

"*Oh, yo té amo,*" she spoke, as she settled deeper in his strong arms, and reached forward with her head and pressed her wet lips against his. She closed her eyes again, and felt his strong presence next to her warm body.

"Oh, alma miå," she exclaimed, "Chu are my hero, chu are my roca. Yo té amo, mucho! I love you so very, very much. make love with me, alma!"

Bart was eagerly responding, with a tenderness in his action and his heart, as the sun was now almost fully awake.

A hearty, old time, ranch breakfast was closely followed by the departure of Bart and Rosalita, back toward the town.

Once the wagon was ready and Rosa started to climb in, she found it ever so difficult to disengage from the clutches of little Annie's hands from off her skirt.

"Leetle Ahnee, eet ees not for chu to *llorar.* Please do not cry, dear one, for soon we shall be back again. Chu must be good for your *abuela y abuelo.*"

"Annie and Tombo," Bart spoke to both, "your Rosa and I will be back to see you soon, and what we want is for you both to be good for your grandmother and grandfather. There is a lot of fun things for you to see and do here on the ranch, and I know you'll keep busy. We'll say adîos for a little while, and we will return, soon."

Bart was very emphatic when he stated this, and he looked them both in the eye, as he pursed to the team to start on.

"Don't look back at them, Rosa," Bart said," It's tough enough to see the roadway straight ahead, and we have to decide when we will come back for a visit to see them again."

The team Bart was driving arrived at the livery stable with he and Rosa at about mid-morning. Bart drove the team over to the corral where he and Walker had all their horses temporarily boarded, and there he returned the rented outfit.

There was Walker Barnes, waiting for Bart with a big grin on his face.

"Wal," he drawled, "ah reckon y'all are gonna have to putt-up with me. Ah've dee-cided to 'company y'all over to yore rainch in Hartley county."

"*Ah, yo estoy muy feliz,*" cried Rosa. "i ahm so hoppy, eet . . ."

"That's great," interrupted Bart. "I'm proud, and I know my folks will be mighty pleased. If we start right away, we'll make it there in time for supper."

The entourage was ready in about fifteen minutes. Bart bought two pack-mules from the livery, and he and Rosa loaded all their goods in the panniers.

Walker rode the big paint horse he'd captured from the Kiowas, and haltered the other two Indian ponies along. The west Texas weather was changing with the hour and Rosalita pulled her *bufanda* closer around her neck and turned up the collar of her outer coat.

The wind was the most menace for the three, and Walker was busy keeping his horses in line, while Bart was managing to control the pack mules.

*   *   *

Walker saw them first, actually, his horses noticed them first. Seven redskins were well mounted and racing toward Bart and the pack mules. Walker quickly reined his pony around and gathered his extra horses, dismounted, and pulled them over and behind some outcropping of boulders.

Bart yelled at Rosalita to follow Walker, and do it now! Bart was about to get both the mules with the rest of the group, but four arrows found their way into one of the mules and he fell over - dead.

Walker was firing his carbine at the onrushing front two warriors, and hit one in his arm. It was one he used to hold a lance, his other arm and shoulder and his chest was semi-protected with his three-skin, stretched shield.

The brave lost his grip on his lance and it fell harmlessly and skidded into one of the big boulders. He had his bow strung across his shoulder and he was trying to retrieve it and notch an arrow, but was in distress with his other wounded arm.

The other Indian, a mean appearing, painted devil, was already loosing his arrows toward Walker, and managed to let fly six or seven before turning his horse to ride past the rock redoubt. It was just luck that none struck the brave cowboy.

Bart was about twenty yards farther along the side of a hill and Rosa was behind him. She had her mare and Bart's and Walker's horses well secured in back of some larger boulders. She had no way to get the other mule, who was still alive. Bart let his halter rope go when the first mule went down. It was standing in the front, alone.

CHAPTER 28

The Indian Walker shot in the arm, was dismounted and crouching behind some rocks about twenty-five yards below the three. He was awkwardly attempting to shoot arrows by drawing his bow with his arm that was wounded, and not finding the mark; he was worse when he switched arms.

Walker couldn't see the other Indian but he did know where the wounded one was, so he directed his firepower at him.

Bart made a decision to go after the mule that was stranded, and standing in front of their rocky obstructions. One of the reasons the mule didn't move was, he was still secured with his lead rope to the halter of the downed mule. Obviously, they were stable mates, and he'd decided he wasn't leaving the other mule.

Bart raced out and down about thirty yards to where the mules were, and sliced the rope free of the other halter. Just as he was starting back to the rocks with the mule, the other five Indians appeared about two hundred yards away.

Bart wanted to remove the panniers from the little, dead mule, because most of their extra ammunition and another rifle and two side guns were packed in there.

There just was not going to be time, and besides, he was having a difficult time getting th other mule to accompany him to the safety of the boulders.

Rosalita could see the Indians, and she heard therm screaming obscenities and whooping as they rode. One of the braves had an old Army musket that he must have found, and stopped his pony to line up a sight to fire it. When he did this, Rosa took careful aim with the Spencer rifle she carried in her scabbard, and fired at him.

She hit the warrior's horse in its shoulder, causing it to rear-up and spin away, unseating the brave at once. Bart saw him and fired a deadly shot that blew a hole through his chest, killing him instantly.

Three of the other four immediately turned their horses around, and the other raced his pony forward to get his fallen comrade.

Bart chased the other little mule up to the rocks where Rosa could catch him. He still felt he had to retrieve both the saddle panniers from the dead mule, so he knelt beside it and started to work fast.

He got the ropes on the first side undone, and slid the packs half-off. He was trying to reach underneath to loosen the second side when, once again, the warriors mounted another furious raid on the group.

One Indian was dead and another two were injured, yet the remaining braves kept up their barrage of arrows, hoping to strike one of their enemy and cause them to quit. Walker inched his way closer to where Rosalita was in order to afford Bart some cover while he gathered their goods from the panniers on the dead mule. Bart finally worked the bags loose, and turned and fired his pistol at the chargers.

Walker and Rosa were shooting their carbines at the oncoming red devils, and one or more of their shots hit another of the braves, toppling him dead, from his horse. This caused the rest to suddenly disburse without even trying to retrieve his body, amid cheers from Rosalita. Bart was relieved that no one was struck with any arrows, and so was Walker.

They all regretted the loss of their little black mule, but were extolling the good news that the rest of the animals survived with no problems. Bart was not certain the Indians had abandoned them, but he was pleased and thank- ful they had seen fit to withdraw their force.

"Y'all s'pose them red-sticks er-a comin' back fer us, Bart?" Walker wanted to know.

"Doubt they will," he replied, "we hurt them pretty bad," "We must leave now, my hosban'" Rosa exclaimed. "While eet ees still light, an we can see ahead . . .an before they come back . . . oh, Bart, are we safe? Will they return again?"

"No, sweetheart, I think that was just a small hunting party that came upon us and decided they would kill us to keep us from their hunting grounds. They won't be back this way, they'd have to cross the Canadian each time, which is what we have to do in about a mile from here."

By this time, Walker had all all animals ready to leave,

They reached the Canadian river and forded in a spot without too much difficulty.

Walker had utilized one of the Indian ponies as an extra pack horse, and to his surprise, the horse reacted with a very small reluctance. It was obvious, now, the horse may have been used for that same purpose at one time or another. He probably pulled a travois, although that was not what Walker wanted him to do.

"It should only be about ten more miles to the ranch," Bart joyously said, when he reached across the saddle pommel and placed his hand on Rosa as she rode against his side.

"*Yo estoy muy excitåtiøn,* so much, how you say, ex-ite-ment," Rosa admitted.

Bart just smiled and shook his head in amazement, that the debacle in which they just took part, afforded them no damages. "Tell you the truth, Rosa, I feel the excitement myself. I recognize so much of this territory, even though it's been a while . . . it doesn't seem to change. I know that my ma'am and my pap are sure going to be happy to finally meet you, and welcome Walker, to boot."

A harsh fall brought on an early start for the coming winter, and as the day sped along, a fierce wind surrounded them all.

The upper edge of the 'llano estado' was particularly vulnerable to severe weather changes. Today was no exception.

When they forded the Canadian river the water was icy cold, and crystals were forming against the northwest banks.

It was time to stop and put on more clothing before they continued the rest of the way in any distress.

Walker unrolled another coat that was tied in back of his saddle, and lifted his neckerchief a lot higher on his face, covering most of it.

Bart had an extra woolen lined vest he quickly put on under his great coat, and he helped Rosalita with her woolen serape and another linsey-wooly shirt for her to wear.

CHAPTER 29

Elstun was finished with the milking chore and brought the separator pieces into the kitchen so they could be cleaned and boiled to get ready for the next use.

"Thatchu, Elstun?" Kate inquired.

"Yeah, hit is, hon," he replied.

"When yore finished up with the milk machine, I wished you'd brang them bitty pieces to the kitchen an boil 'em out. I'm a'ready startin' mah sewin' fer this evenin', Els, an ahm all sot down with Elizabeth in chere by the far place."

"Ah've already done thet, Kate," Elstun answered, "an ahm a-brangin' in a heap more far-wood. Hit's a-gittin' a-right more airish outside."

Elstun propped the kitchen door open so he could carry in a big arm load of fire wood, and while the door was open, both Dusty and Biff, his outside hounds, bounded in and made a direct line for the room where the fire was crackling.

The two hounds made such a racket when they entered the room, it caused Kate's cat, to leap from the warm, cozy confines of her lap, and scatter a dress and paper pattern Kate was working on, all over the floor.

"Yar, you dag-gum dawgs! You come a-tarryhootin' in mah house, and skeer the fool outta 'Elizabeth, an cause her to swarve outen mah lap an upsot everthin' I been a-sewin' on in chere," she hollered.

When the cat leapt from Kate's lap she not only tangled the sewing-in-progress, she accidentally knocked over the white, porcelain ash tray, Kate used constantly. This action bumped out the lit cigarette resting in the tray, where it fell to the floor under Kate's chair, out of sight.

Kate was so busy re-gathering her sewing and her patterns and needle and threads, she failed to notice the upset ash tray with the lighted cigarette.

"Ah, Kate," Elstun said, "I'll hep you redd-up. Them ol' dawgs don't chouse that cat. She jes spooks easy, is all."

The two were on their hands and knees, picking up all the spilled thread and papers and materials Kate was busy with when they met one another head-on, crawling toward each other, and they both began to chuckle, then laugh uproariously.

Biff, the red-bone hound, simply couldn't stand it any more, and ran over to both of them and began licking their faces. Dusty just went to sleep beside the fireplace.

"Er, Kate," Elstun spoke, as he stood up and placed some material on her chair, "I've got to give-down to ya fer me a-lettin' them dawgs run in, and ahm rat sorry they caused 'Lizabeth to mess up yore doin's." He placed his muscled arm around her shoulder, and lifted her chin to meet her lips with his, and tenderly kissed her, while she ardently kissed him back.

"Oh, Lordy," she cried out, as she backed away from the kitchen with an empty milk pail full of pump water, and poured it on the burning, hand-hooked rug.

Half an hour later, Kate and Elstun had forgotten the rug-fire incident, and were settled nicely enjoying the heat put forth from their stone fireplace.

The darkness of evening brought more of the fierce winds that howl across this upper corner of the Texas panhandle, and the two found themselves raising their voices in order to be heard in their conversations.

"Elstun," Kate spoke first, as she looked up from her sewing.

"Whut is it, Kate?" he answered.

"Seems as like I heered horses a-nickerin', jes this minute . . . or is it the evils, or is it thet dern whisperin' Injun, again? You hear it, Els?"

"Ah reckon ah do, sweet-gum. You jes sit tight, an ah'll see to it."

Biff and Dusty both raised their lazy bones and left the warmth of the fireplace, and headed to the front door. This time they weren't growling . . . but they were both whining and pawing at the door sill. When Elstun arrived, he neck-chained the dogs, and opened the door.

"Lord have mercy," cried Elstun, as he stepped outside. Hit's them, Kate, they're here at last, now come quick."

Kate was out the door and on to the porch in seconds, shouting her joy aloud.

"Glory, be, Barton Dan'l," she said."

"Step down and give yore ma'am a hug."

Bart was already dismounted and he was helping his somewhat apprehensive wife to dismount, also.

"Hello, Momma, howdy, Dad. It's mighty good to be here. Bart reached out and gave his mother a crushing hug, and a big kiss, and reached over and threw his arms around his father's shoulders, before the two shook hands.

"Look here, you two, this is Rosalita, my loving new wife, isn't she beautiful? Isn't she everything I wrote you about?" Bart was nervous, but not half as nervous as Rosa.

Kate hugged Rosalita, and Elstun started to do the same, but stopped just as he saw Kate glance toward him. He reached out and grabbed her hand and furiously shook it.

"Ahm mighty proud to make yore acquaintance," he jabbered.

"Oh, *mucho güsto,* Señor Cal-hoon," Rosalita replied, as she curtsied. "My great plea-sure," she repeated in English. "And chu are just as beautiful as my hos-ban said you would be, *Señora,"* smiling and nodding to Kate.

"Daddy," Bart spoke, as he motioned for Walker to step forward. "Mother, this is Walker Barnes." Bart was all smiles and as proud as if the cowboy was his own brother, when he introduced him to both his parents. "He's visiting with us for a while, and I have something else to tell you when we get inside. Walker howdy'd them both, and shook hands, too.

"I'll take care of all the animals," Walker said, as he gathered them and headed for the barn. "Bart, y'all go on with yore folks now, ya heah? I'll be up thar directly," Walker replied.

Biff and Dusty were almost beside themselves, after they determined that Bart was someone that returned from their past, that they both new and recalled, and kept jumping up and wanting to be petted and remembered. Bart lovingly complied.

"Let's get our-sel's inside," Elstun remarked, "Hit's near 'bout as cold as it were last night, and that were cold 'nuf to freeze-up the warter truffs."

"Thar's a nice far a-goin' and you kin warm up yoursel's afore you putt up all yore belongings." Kate spoke to the pair. "C'mon, honey, I'll hep you settle-in," she directed to Rosalita, while taking her arm, and one of her parcels.

The four moved inside with Elstun urging the dogs on ahead, watching as they made their way back in front of the roaring fire. Elizabeth was totally undisturbed by the commotion, continuing to lie curled-up on Kate's chair, and feigning a deep sleep.

Moments later, Walker came in with one of the panniers and the extra weapons.

"Bart," he whispered quietly aside after he entered. "Ah thank you and I art to go get the rest of the gear, rat, now." Walker emphatically nodded and motioned with his head. "If y'all will pardon us," he said.

"Bart, sumpthin's mighty strange. There's three Injuns camped behind the barn."

CHAPTER 30

Bart and Walker cautiously made their way toward the back end of the barn with their pistols drawn. Bart finally saw what Walker was talking about when he saw the two buffalo hides that were tied together to make a 'lean-to' cover at the back side of the building.

There were two horses standing hip-shot next to a small, almost unseen, cook fire. Bart approached from one side and the cowboy, from the other.

It appeared to Bart that two of the figures crouched under the hide cover were women. The other, standing nearer the fire, was a man.

"All right," Bart said aloud, "step over here in front of me, and keep your hands together. What are you doing here?"

At that moment, Walker stepped out of the shadows and mentioned them to move by waving his pistol. "Move," he said.

The two women huddled together and the man stepped in front of them, raised his arm, palm out, and spoke.

"You are '*Aht-sa-té*'," he said. "you are known as 'Young Rabbit Cal-hoon'. You make long journey, gone many, winter, not see home camp for long time. You n . . ."

"Whisperin' Charlie! That you? Well, I'll be-" Bart interrupted. Put your gun away, Walker, this man is an old and good friend . . . he's known me and my folks for many years. He's a reservation Indian that my daddy pulled out of some bog about ten years ago, and he visits my folks once in a while . . . usually for a handout. What are you doin' here, Charlie? Who are these two squaws?"

"Tuc-su 'na ahté, or Flower at Spring, wife of Charlie and mother of *Ya-nå,* who is known as Blue Flower, once a wife of sub chief of Black Water clan of Kwhadie. Wel-com', Young Rabbit," Charlie answered.

"I don't know what you all are doing here," Bart questioned, "but I'm glad to see you, and so will my folks be. C'mon up to the house, we're all going to have some food, and you'll be welcome, too."

"I'll tell you about this Charlie fella," Bart said to Walker, as they all started toward the ranch house. "He's an Apache, from the Mescalero tribe over in New Mexico, and he captured this Comanche girl when on a raid."

"The Comanches caught him and a hunting party he was with later, and spared his life when they found he'd taken the girl, a younger sister of an old war chief, for his wife. In an exchange for his life, he agreed to scout for the Kwhadie. He and six or seven other families finally left for the reservation. That's when I first got to know him. My dad pulled him out of some bog while he was looking for his steers, over near the reservation."

The five reached the house, but the two women stayed outside, against the lee side of the front porch, afraid to enter a house.

Whisperin' Charlie followed Bart and Walker to the door, and was greeted by Elstun, coming to look for the men.

"Whisperin' Charlie, what brings you around these parts agin?" Elstun inquired, surprised to see him and the two Indian women beside the porch steps. "Don't tell me them Comanch' is runnin' round chere, an ah see you run into

Aht-sa-té, ain't that whut you named him? He's come home fer a spell, Charlie."

"Charlie go. You no fear Kwhadie, they south-east. Charlie take *Tuc-Su-na-até* and *Ya-Nå to* land of Mescalero, my people, to the west at first light. Need one horse, one blanket and to-bac-o. We go at first light in morning. Don't forget whuskey."

"Wal, ain't that jes like him," Els said to his son. "You 'member he was always a-comin' and a-goin', quick as a bird. Ah 'spec we kin let him have the blanket and the tobacky, and some whusky - but, he cain't take no hoss, at's fer shore."

"Mistah Calhoon," Walker spoke up. "I allow as how he kin take that liver and white spotted pony I brought along. I really got no use fer him, and 'sides, I got them other ones. I'm jes sarten it's Kiowa broke, and it'd jes be one more I'd have to put shoes on. Another thing," he continued, "he's smooth-mouthed, anyway."

An old horse mattered not to Charlie as long as he had some food in his belly, some tobacco in his pouch, an extra blanket to keep his legs warm, and especially, whiskey to keep his insides warm.

Supper, enjoyed by all together, except the Indians, who would not enter the house, was soon over. Bart explained the position of Walker, who, well able to speak for himself, had his cause championed by his friend, Bart.

He explained how he'd more or less promised the cowboy a job on this ranch, with the understanding that he would be able to lighten the load for Elstun, and develop a horse herd that could help the ranch make some good money in only a few months. He would also help with the range management for the cattle units, which would also increase monthly earnings shortly.

"Ah thank hit's a excellent idee, son," Kate replied. "Whatta you thank, Elstun?"

"Oh, you betcha," he answered with a broad grin on his face. "Ah've allus had a figurin' this spread could pay off, with all the good grass, an a little extry help."

Walker was particularly pleased with the decisions made, and let it be known that he would start by acquiring several good brood mares he knew about from the livery manager back in Amarillo. His next question was where he could find a good stallion that could develop a foundation stud, and that question was soon answered when Elstun said he knew of one.

"Ol' Jake Ellis has that five-year old he brought out with him last year from Arkansas. he's the best in these ol' parts that I know of, and Jake still owes me fer all that wood I cut fer him when he was laid-up last winter. He'll sell us that stud o'his'n, fer shore."

While the men were still discussing their plans for ranch management, Kate and Rosalita were busy acquainting themselves with one another.

Kate was fascinated with Rosalita. She had never been associated with or ever really known a Mexican señora, and she kept staring at her, causing a trace of embarrassment for Rosa. However, it was being enacted too, by Rosa.

There was no trace of the Indians when the men appeared at first light to start their morning chores.

"Look here," said Walker, as he approached the barn. "That there Injun must'a drank all his whusky last night, fer he plumb fergot to take that 'ere paint hoss ah said he could have."

"Shore 'nuf," exclaimed Elstun.

"I expect he new exactly what he was doing," Bart replied. "Whisperin' Charlie is a pretty smart Indian. He's an Apache, and is returning his allegiance to his people. The horse is Kiowa, and would bring bad medicine to the Apache.

They would likely torture them after they shot the horse and ate it, just because it was Kiowa bred. The Kiowa and Comanche are bitter enemies of the Apache. My guess is,

Charlie rides one horse and his other one packs all their possibles, and his wife and daughter walk to New Mexico. That seems to be the standard mores of life in the Indian nations, least what I've been informed," Bart stated.

"Ah reckon ah kin trade them Injun ponies with a little boot, fer them mares in Ameriller, next week," Walker stated.

CHAPTER 31

Tombo and little Annie were two healthy youngsters, and their grand-folks were seeing to their needs very well. Lucy Crawford had been in touch with the school teacher in town, and had made arrangements for the children to start attending classes.

Since it was about four miles to the school house from the Crawford place, it was fitting that Noah arrange to harness a gentle horse to the buggy for the kids to drive to school. This was one of many rigs that were driven to the school by students. Some rode horseback, too, but they were all placed in corals for the six hours of daily classes.

It wasn't too many days before Tombo was able to harness the gelding to the buggy, and learn to care for him while he was tethered or turned loose in the school corral.

His grandfather was very proud of him, and Annie, too, for that matter. She always saw to it that the morrall bag was available with oats.

While every effort was made for the comfort and care of Annie and Tombo, when school was over and chores were done, and the evening meal was finished, there were many un- answered questions that they wondered about and left them with dreams of their parents, especially dreams about their mother.

Moreover, they still missed being with Bart and Rosalita; after all, they had been constant companions ever since that first day they boarded the stage coach and started their arduous journey.

Grandma Lucy was very cognizant of this situation, and felt it would help a great deal if either they took both the children to visit the Calhoon ranch, or hopefully, Bart and Rosa would visit the Crawfords soon. The bright side of the picture for the youngsters was the fact that they could play with and be around other children at their school.

There were fourteen children at this school. One of two, it was located on the north side of town. The other school enrolled seventy-two.

*   *   *

Elstun was telling Walker about his Indian friend, Whispirin' Charlie, and of the strange ways he sometimes displayed.

"You know," Bart said, while speaking with Walker and his dad, "this Charlie is a whole lot smarter than you might think. Even though he appears reserved and stoic it's only his . . ."

"He's a powerful good tracker," said Elstun, interrupting. "an 'at's fer shore."

"One of the courses I studied at college was on Indian language interpretation and convinced me of the superior intelligence of the Apache Indian nation as compared with other tribes of American Indians," Bart said, further.

"We saved them books you sent us, Bart. They's in the big ol' box by yore bed," Elstun injected into the conversation.

Bart continued. "Many of the African, Australian and North and South American tribes can't count beyond ten, but the Apaches count to ten thousand as easily as we do."

Elstun looked rather perplexed.

"With us the number one has no correlative. When we come to two, we say two, twelve, twenty, two hundred; with three, we say thirteen, thirty, three hundred, and so on.

"In Apache, one is called *tash-ay-ay*; two is *nah-kee;* three, *kay-yay;* four is *tin-yay;* five is *asht-lay;* six, *host-kon-ay*; seven is *host-ee-day*; eight, *hah-pee*; nine, *en-gost-ay,* and ten is *go-nay-nan-ay."*

"Whew!, at's remarkable, son," Elstun said.

"Ahm surprised you remember all that there larnin'. Does Rosey know you savvy all thet'ere 'Pache talk? Walker posed this question to his friend.

"I remember that thirty is called *kah-tin-yay,* and forty is *tish-ti-yay,* and fifty is *asht- tin-yay.* One hundred is *too-ooh,* and two hundred is *nah-kee-too-ooh.*

"Some more of the Apache language," Bart continued, "is interesting, for when he says, *shee,* he means I or me, and *dee-dah* means you. When an object is shown them for the first time, they adopt its Spanish name along with their guttural, *hay.* The name for iron is *pesh,* Silver, *pesh-lickolee,* or white iron, and gold is *pesh-klitso,* or yellow iron.

In adapting the Spanish, silver was *plata-hay,* and gold was *oro-hay.* They call white men *Pindah-Lickoyee,* or 'White-eyes'."

"Ah remember you a-tellin' us you fit them 'Paches once or twice, when you was with the Army over in New Mexico," said Walker, "but ah didn't know you savvied their talk."

"Well," mused Bart, "you almost have to keep in practice, or you're liable to forget. I can tell you that their women are very chaste. For a while, when many were under our charge, and mingling with our troops, not a single case occurred where an Apache woman surrendered herself to any man outside her tribe, and infidelity is extremely rare among them."

"Just about the exact opposite is true with the Navajo or the Kiowa and the Comanche. I've heard tell that the Navajo women are extremely loose and sensuous."

"Ah'll tell you boys, right now," Walker spoke up," they ain't no way I'd ever be of a mind to romance one o' them red-sticks, no siree, Bob!"

"Let's have a look at your work team, Daddy," Bart said to his father. "You still usin' Rafe and ol' Dan?"

"Oh, you betcha, they's a powerful team, son, and they's gentle 'nuf that Kate kin work 'em. That is, if'n she's a mind to."

The trio made their way to the barn for a good look at the huge horses that did the heavy work on the ranch. "You're sartin' them boys kin heist a load?" Walker said, with tongue in cheek, to Elstun, "their feet look kinda dainty."

The fact was, Elstun had never shod these draft horses, but he did keep their hoofs trimmed, and rasped back when they grew. They had good, big feet thet would require special, forge-shaped horse shoes of the largest size.

This was a task Elstun could perform if he decided to ever put shoes on them.

CHAPTER 32

The evening firelight was casting shadows in the otherwise, dimly lit room where Bart was holding Rosalita in his arms on the long sofa facing the fireplace.

He was reminiscing aloud some of his past memories of his earlier days spent on the ranch, while Rosa was enthralled with his dialogue of events.

"Chu must have missed thees life very much, my hosban, while een the Army and then working so hard down een Presidio, een the cotton-meel."

"Not so fast, darlin'," he said. "I would have never met you, if I hadn't been in south Texas, and that meeting was the most important one in my life."

"Oh, Bart, *alma mîa,* we have gone through a lot together in such a short time, and chu have been won-der-ful for me. I must tell you how very much I miss the *niños,* those children, leetle Annie and *chico,* Tombo."

"Well, I do too, Rosa, I miss them very much. I guess I got mighty used to them, bein' 'round them all the time. And especially after what they endured. . . .Are you thinking what I'm thinking, alma?"

"*Si,* oh, yes, yes. We must visit to them tomorrow," Rosa replied. "I can be ready to leave een the early time. We can take the buggy, and perhaps the Cra-fords weel allow us to stay a leetle while."

"All right," Bart agreed, "I'll talk with my folks and we'll arrange to visit the children tomorrow. I'm certain we can stay several days."

Morning found Bart and Rosalita at the buggy, hitched and ready to visit the Crawfords and the children. Walker Barnes was busy at the barn starting to shoe the work team, as Elstun and Kate approached the buggy and it's sorrel horse.

"Here's ye some lunch in this here ol' basket that I packed fer y'all. Have a nice trip and if'n you decide to brang them little ones back here fer a visit, why, you knowed you'd be welcome," Kate remarked, as she bade them farewell.

The trip back to Amarillo was not as difficult as the trip from there to the Calhoon ranch had been; it seemed to take a little less time. The weather was more mild, and a sense of urgency was absent.

Bart drove the horse under the tall poles at the entrance to the Crawford ranch, and headed for the main house.

Tombo was helping his grandfather at the barn when he saw the buggy approach. He immediately recognized Rosa and Bark and ran toward the buggy to greet them.

Noah, suffering from failing eyesight, had to rely on Tombo to tell him who it was at that distance, and he was pleased.

School was out for the day, and the evening chores were about to be started, so while Rosa visited with Annie and her grandmother, Bart accompanied Tombo and his grandfather to lighten their tasks.

There was no question that the children missed Bart and Rosa, they clung to them like static on a wool skirt, and begged to stay up a little later after supper was over, so they could be with them for an even longer time.

The next morning the ladies decided to drive the children to school in the ranch wagon and have Rosalita meet their teacher. Then the two ladies would do a bit of shopping in the town stores. Annie wasn't too happy with that decision, she wanted to go with Rosalita. They assured her they'd be back when her school was over and take them both back to the ranch. Tombo couldn't talk his grandparents into letting him miss school either, and he finally resolved to go.

About midmorning, Sheriff Towne and his deputy rode into the Crawford ranch and stepped down to talk with Noah. When Bart spotted the sheriff, one of his first questions was what had become of Martin Carrington.

The sheriff, happy to see Bart, explained that Carrington was fit to stand trial and it was scheduled to start in two days.

He told Bart that since he was here, it would save him a trip to serve a summons to appear in the court for testimony in the case, which he figured was civil and not take very long.

Several days later, at the trial, Bart heard the testimony of the various witnesses, and told what he knew of the episode. He found out that the black bag that Carrington always kept with him contained cash of which he would use to put fresh capital in the company, to stave off the imminent bankruptcy.

He also found out that Jason Crawford's sidekick supplied the money from various bank robberies, after skimming from the cash to Carrington in promise of a silent partnership in the company, provided they could keep the railroad away.

All this, of course went awry, when Jason was slain, and Carrington was found out, arrested, then tried and convicted.

Pat Packard, the bank manager, was now more eager than ever to have Lynx Walters become involved with the stage line, and arranged a final meeting with Lynx and consolidated the transaction.

When Bart would eventually return to the Calhoon ranch, he'd tell Walker all about the mystery of Carrington's famous black valise.

The morning of the day Bart and Rosalita were getting ready to leave to return to the Calhoon ranch, a disaster caused a terrible turn of events.

For sometime Noah Crawford's eyesight had given him a tremendous amount of trouble. He was a proud man and he tried to hide the fact his eyes were deteriorating; however, Lucille was quite cognizant of the fact they were.

Tombo was beside himself with grief as he ran, screaming, toward the house.

"Bart, Bart," he sobbed, "sumpthin bad's the matter with Grandpa Noah, hurry, he's at the barn." Tombo had been helping his grandfather with some morning chores, as he usually did before eating breakfast and getting ready for school.

Bart, sensing the urgency in the lad's voice, raced ahead to the barn to find the trouble. At first, he thought Noah was just standing at the other end of the barn, until he came closer and called out his name. There was no answer.

Somehow, Noah had inadvertently walked into the noose end of the long rope attached to the block and tackle, used to hoist the bales of hay into the the loft atop the barn, where they were stored until needed.

The pull of the rope, when Noah stumbled into it, caused the counterbalanced weight of the block and tackle to instantly fall from the loft, raising the noosed end to pull upward.

The weight only lifted Noah a very short way off the ground, but it was just enough to jerk his neck in a gruesome way and snap the life from this kind old man.

It was this that Tombo must have witnessed, and caused him unmeasurable hurt and anxiety, compounding his fear of what other hardships he could endure.

Bart acted quickly, but it was too late to save the affable patriarch.

The events that followed were truly difficult, under the circumstances that prevailed. Aside from the grieving that was done, an orderly administration for burial had to be accomplished. Rosa was a tremendous asset to Bart while he handled the arrangements, aiding in the comfort of Lucy and the children.

Word traveled fast in the growing city of Amarillo, especially among the ones that knew and respected old Noah Crawford.

They remembered him as a man who'd been through more then the average person, with the notoriety of his son, and they remembered him as a respected veterinarian.

Services were arranged and interment was in the church yard next to where his son was buried. That week-end, before Bart and Rosalita finally were preparing to return to the Calhoon ranch, Lucille Crawford made a very special announcement to them.

"I've decided to sell the ranch," she said, "and move in with my younger sister, Margaret. She's a widow, too, you know, and her home in town will be far easier for us both to keep up with."

"Well, Missus Crawford," Bart spoke up, "if you're certain your mind's made up, I don't suppose there's any chance of changing it."

This ranch was getting to be a little too much for you both this last year according to what Noah told me, and so I guess it's for the best."

"It's only a section of land," Lucy said, "but it's got good water and grass, and we're only running about forty mother cows on it. Mister Hal Denlinger's been coming over to help Noah out with the herd, and I expect he would look after them until I am able to sell; Bart, would you be . . . ?"

"It's a fine spread, Mis' Crawford, and I know what you're thinking. I still have some ties to a job in south Texas, and . . . besides, what will become of your grandchildren if you move in with your sister, in town?"

"I have thought on it, Bart, and as sad as it is, I'd have to let Mrs. Stark keep them at her home for children. I'd send her a monthly stipend, of course, but there's just no way, especially now, that I can care for them daily."

Bart's reaction was a solemn pause before he spoke, and said, "You know, Mis' Crawford, I'd like to think this over and especially talk with Rosalita. Do you suppose you could take care of the youngsters for several more days? We'll make a quick trip to my folks' ranch and both be back this Saturday."

"I guess you're anxious to settle something, and for the sake of Tombo and Annie, we all should make an effort to consider their welfare."

That said, Bart headed for the house to get Rosa and gather their bags, and bid farewell to the children. He made certain they understood he and Rosa would return the coming week end.

CHAPTER 33

The buggy drive to the Calhoon ranch was shortened in time by the length of the conversation between the two, seasoned, newly-weds, in a serious and excited mood.

" . . . and actually," Bart continued to tell Rosa, "That job of mine down in Presidio will keep. I still have another five months of my sabbatical left before I need to discuss my future with them."

"I not chure what chu mean, my hos-ban, about the Sabbath, bot I theenk chu mean by that, chu have some time free to go to *Iglesia*- ..to- church ¿Chess?" "Never mind," he answered, "Missus Crawford wants $8,000. for the ranch, including all the livestock, and house. Minus her belongings, of course."

"I not know if eet ees good to do thees, bot if chu wish, I weel follow what ever chu say. Oh, Bart, ¿what weel hoppen to the children, they are *muchachas pequeño,* still leetle?"

"That's the second thing I want to discuss with you, my love. What would you think if we could adopt the children, buy the Crawford ranch, and settle down there and raise a family?"

By now, Bart had pulled rein on the buggy horse, and stopped along the road to get a full reaction from Rosalita.

She reacted immediately by throwing her arms around her husband and kissing him fervently and arduously.

Bart explained to Rosa the reason behind his consideration to take the children. The decision by their grandmother to live in town with her sister, and for their well being, foremost. he felt certain he and Rosa could soon make the ranch into a prosperous and very fruitful enterprise.

Not to mention, it would be reasonably close to his parents' ranch over in Hartley county, and Walker Barnes, too.

"There's bound to be a passel of things to be worked out if we can make this happen," Bart remarked, "so, I'm anxious to start."

Rosalita was almost in a state of euphoria; she was so pleased with the decisions they both agreed upon. She was now in as much of a hurry to reach the Calhoun ranch, and return to Amarillo, as was her husband. The rest of the way she only talked of making all kinds of plans, especially where little Annie and Tombo were in the picture.

"We can move that large cabinet that stands in the hallway at your mother . . ."

"Take it easy, sweetheart," Bart told her, "we haven't even offered to buy the ranch from Lucy Crawford yet. We'd have to come to an agreement, and then I need to talk with Pat Packard at the bank about a mortgage on the ranch, and . . ."

"Oh, I know, my hos-ban, but chu can, how-you-say, 'work eet out'. ¿What weel your parents theenk, especially about us taking *los niños en los paternidad,?* Rosa playfully questioned Bart.

"What will they think of us being parents to Annie and Tombo? Ha!. they'll be downright happy for us - you'll see."

A short while after Bart and Rosa arrived at the Calhoon ranch, all the explanations were given and discussed among the four adults. Bart decided to return to Amarillo in a few days, and thought that Rosa should be with him.

In the meantime, the young Calhoons enjoyed their stay at the ranch, together with a solidifying bonding between Kate and Rosalita - much to Barts approval.

Kate and Elstun were totally pleased with the decision that was made to adopt the children, and also to buy the Crawford ranch.

"I've knowed thet rainch fer some time, Bart, and hit's a powerful good place to put down a family and run ye a few cows."

Elstun was serious with his son, and also pleased they would be a lot nearer to home, even over in Amarillo. Kate felt they they would surely see more of each other as soon as the purchase was arranged.

Bart said he had a little over one thousand dollars saved in the Stockman's bank in Presidio, but he'd have to wire for the money when he got to Amarillo.

Elstun told Bart that he should ask that Pat Packard feller how much his bank would loan on the Crawford place, and that he and his mother could lend him about six hundred dollars.

Bart told his dad he would check out all the possible ways that he and Rosa could buy the Crawford ranch . . . if the final price was what he could afford.

Rosa informed them that no matter if they bought the Crawford ranch or not, it was her wish they make sure they could *adoptør,* -adopt- the children . . . even if they had to take them back to south Texas.

When the young Calhoons arrived in Amarillo, they went to see the banker to ask for the deal to be worked out to buy the ranch they wanted. Pat Packard had already secured the necessary paperwork to approve the transaction, and Lucille Crawford was willing to sell the ranch to Bart and Rosa for five hundred dollars less, if they would care for the children.

Lucille Crawford was not yet aware, nor was Bart and Rosalita, that steps had been taken by the county attorney, through the courts, to approve the adoption of the Crawford children.

Part of the result was due to the effort of the children's teacher, whose cousin just happened to be the attorney for Potter county.

Everything was working out for the best for Rosa and Bart. The bank was very willing to hold a mortgage for six thousand, and that left only one hundred dollars short of the amount needed for the bank to loan eighty percent of the selling price.

Bart wired his bank in Presidio for the one thousand, and Elstun produced his six hundred. With the selling price lowered to seventy-five hundred, the balance had to equal the agreed amounts.

There was going to be another twenty dollars needed for some closing costs, and eighty dollars for the attorney to file all the paperwork.

About that time, Walker Barnes came riding in past the bank, headed for the livery stable. he had two extra horses with him, and wanted fifty dollars for each one. The farrier at the stable looked them over closely and decided to give him his price. Smiling, Walker rode straight to the bank, where he'd seen Bart talking to the banker as he rode in, and walked inside offering to lend Bart the profits of his 'Injun ponies' sale.

It wasn't long before all the details were finalized, and Bart and Rosa were new owners. The news arrived that the court had awarded them the Crawford children, and a final adoption would be approved next week. All that remained now was for Bart and Rosalita to gather their belongings and move to the ranch house they now owned.

They explained the entire process to Annie and Tombo, and weren't surprised as the youngsters gleefully looked forward to the arrangement.

One of the happiest people was young Walker Barnes.

END